Hemingway

Hemingway

*A Collection of Stories based on
the Album of the Same Name*

DAN JOHNSON
TRAVIS ERWIN

For information contact

Editor@Barbadum Books

or visit

www.BarbadumBooks.com

Cover and Photo Art by LoudMouth Visual Works
Cover Design by Izzy is Dead Records

ISBN: 978-0-692-93654-2

First Edition: July 2018

10 9 8 7 6 5 4 3 2 1

For Dan's Father ...

Terry Wayne Johnson, US Air Force. Born
Mar. 1, 1954. Lost to suicide, Dec. 6, 1987.

Dad I know it wasn't your fault.
I know you thought you were doing me a favor.
I love you. I forgive you.
And I'm doing the best thing I know how to
do with it.

See you some time soon, man.

An Introduction ...
from Walt Wilkins

My friend Dan Johnson is a serious man with a big voice and a good heart.

His new project, record and book together, springs up from deep inside his past and present, and grabs you by your spirit.

Dan sings his stories with conviction, taking the listener through tales of real danger, real life and real salvation. The book features stories with the characters from the songs.

It's ambitious, for sure.

Ambitious, deep, and rewarding. I'm glad Dan and Travis followed this call into the dark and the light.

Right on, brother.

Good work,

WW

Preface

Travis

Good and Evil. The dichotomy of the two words is invariably linked to religion, and quite often, Good is pitted versus Evil in a battle for everlasting supremacy. Or in some religions, the two are said to live in harmony, with one relying on the other. I will leave the theological debates over which philosophy contains more merit to someone else, as my goal was simply to humanize both of these aspects in a variety of ways. Some more subtle than others.

But just as those concepts are at times fuzzy, so too is the story of how I came to be part of this project. It began one morning, when I picked up my phone to turn off the alarm. Mornings and buzzing alarms—now there are two things purely evil. Yet, no one can argue each new day is a gift, thereby making that morning a good thing even when it comes way too early, at the behest of a beckoning job. There's some Yin and Yang for you.

Turning off the alarm, I saw a text from my friend Dan. A text containing the lyrics to a song titled, *Hemingway*. I read the words and thought … *that is the most powerful thing Dan has ever written*. I didn't realize this was a fork in the road for me, but the character in Dan's song set up shop in my head and whispered to me all that day. That's when I knew that I badly wanted … no needed, to write this character's full story. Hoping Dan would let me run with his creation and expand upon it, I set about pleading my case.

Luckily, he liked the idea and I got to work writing Hemingway. What I thought would take a few days took a few months as the character continued to whisper in my ear.

Dan offered more insight into the chracter after an early draft and that is how John Rivero became Hemingway. I did my best to channel the narrative style of Papa himself, and that in itself was an honor for me to attempt.

Later Dan brought me on board to help create the project you are now holding. Dan and I held many talks and meetings. We philosophized over a few dozen stouts and porters, each diving into our own beliefs in regard to good and evil.

The stories relate to the songs they are tied to in different ways. From a prequel approach, to an expanded look at the present, and even a bit of what came after the last lyric so you, the reader and listener, are privy to an expanded look at these characters and their individual dilemmas.

The characters face grave choices and situations, but as a whole this project is about what comes as a result of these choices and how our decisions affect not only us individually, but also those whose paths we cross.

Few people consciously make what they feel are bad or evil choices, but everyone has a different set of guidelines. So what a person feels is a good choice at the time, can lead them to a very bad place. Or a person can make a so-called wrong choice, only to have a serendipitous outcome.

A flip of the coin if you will. And speaking of coins, are there any more infamous than the pieces of silver paid to Judas for the betrayal of Christ?

Historians mostly agree these coins would have been Tyrian shekels. I had some fun as a writer researching the lore around these coins, and much of that research filtered its way into these stories. After all what other coin would the Devil be so willing to bargain for?

Dan

When I was a kid, I actually used to look forward to going to the doctor. Not for the nose-crinkling medicines, definitely not for the needles, not even for the occasional, amply endowed nurse who rested your head on her bosom to comfort you. (Although that's a pretty good reason too, come to think of it.) I enjoyed going because as soon as we'd walk in the door, I'd make a beeline for the *Highlights Magazine*.

I wanted to beat the hidden picture puzzle. I'd borrow a pen from the front desk and hope no other little snot-nosed kid had already marked it up. There was something tremendously gratifying in searching that picture and finding what was hidden in it. One thing morphs into another, some things are flipped backward or upside-down, you're not quite sure what you're looking at until you find it, and it becomes clear. And throughout the whole thing is some clever, common theme.

I suppose when we set out to write this book, that's exactly the kind of spirit I went into it with. We flipped it backward, in reverse chronological order and spent months researching places and characters to fill it with little hidden puzzles. Some of them we "hid" in plain site for everyone to see. Then again some of this is so secretly autobiographical that maybe no one will ever really know how many special, hidden threads are woven between the lines. But I hope you'll find the most important ones. And I hope you'll enjoy it the way I enjoyed those *Highlights Magazines*.

This book is an allegory on the inseparable nature of Good and Evil in this world. And the understanding of humanity's power to make a choice in each moment to manifest that Good or Evil to the best of their ability - with no reliable guarantees of the ultimate outcome.

Basically this Universe may take something we perceive as Evil and make it ultimately work for Good. Conversely, the road to hell is paved with good intentions, as the old adage says. Was the torture and crucifixion of Jesus the Nazarene a Good thing? Was it an Evil thing? It was certainly terrible. But for those of you who identify as Christians around the world, was it a necessary Evil for the Ultimate Good? Can we ever really know in the short-term? So much of this isn't even up to us. All we have is now.

This project really began December 6th, 1987. That was the night my father hanged himself. It was the day before my eleventh birthday. The album and my contribution to this book are dedicated to him and to the families of veterans—fathers and mothers, brothers and sisters, sons and daughters like him, who have felt the grief of loss, magnified by the fact that that loss was chosen and executed by the one we love, left for us to mourn forever.

Dad, it wasn't selfish. I realize you thought you were doing me a favor. I'm doing the best thing I can think of with it.

More recently this all began to take shape one Summer day a few years ago in Key West, Florida, as I stood in the study of Ernest Hemingway, contemplating his genius, his contribution to this world, the man and the character he was in life, and his ultimate death by his own hand. Standing there, I wrote the final line to the song "Hemingway" and built the rest of the lyrics around it later.

Twenty percent of the sales from this book, the accompanying album, and any other sales or profits related to them, will forever go to support the fight against veteran suicide in America.

We encourage you to learn more at ...

www.operationhemingway.org

A Digital Copy of the Album is included with your purchase of this book.

Visit

www.nwdownload.com

and use your personal access code

DJABZHC8VC

The Devil's Child

Inspired by the song "The Favor" by Dan Johnson

Billy was a half-breed.

That wasn't supposed to matter. Not these days. But it did. Even in South Dakota, a state that in its day had seen plenty of half breeds and half truths. Even more so, it mattered to both his dad and to his grandfather. The two men were unlikely to agree water was wet, yet when it came to Billy, and even more so Billy's mom, the two men swam the same turbulent river of regret, hate, and blame.

Way Billy figured, they shared fault for his mother's death. Equally. In halves.

Billy's grandfather lived on the Pine Ridge reservation down in the Badlands, and for a while after his mom died his grandfather made the three hour drive up to Pierre every third weekend. He would take Billy out to eat, or to fish at Lake Oahe, or to just look at something he thought the boy needed to see, to properly understand his heritage.

But court ordered visitations be damned, Billy's father never made it easy, and after months of bickering, threats, and caustic confrontations, the visits petered out to nothing.

"Nothing. That's what those people considered your mom after she married me." Billy's father would punctuate his points with violent hand motions anytime Billy dared mention his Lakota blood.

"They treated her like nothing. Why? Why? Why?" His father would ramp himself into preacher mode and rail powerfully in his baritone. "Because I'm white. Because I believe God. Because I am not ashamed to say so."

That shit was all true enough, but Billy's father was a hypocrite just the same. Because he was just as prideful, just as ready to shame another for their beliefs. Just as prejudiced.

When Billy tried to grow his black hair long like his friend Logan Two Elks, his father bellowed. "Why would you want to wear your hair like some Godless heathen? Why? Why? Why?"

When he smelled weed on Billy, he shouted, "Stay away from that Logan boy! His people are nothing but trouble." The words "his people" spat out like a bad taste.

Logan was never the one who brought the joints down to the church basement. That had been blond-haired, blue-eyed Jack Howard. But no way would his dad blame a boy reared in the shadow of his precious Church of God assembly. No, it had to be Billy's other friend, from the people only a few generations removed from the "savages" that scalped Custer and his men. The lineage of blood-thirsty warriors that fought like hell to fight invaders hungry for gold and for the land that held it, simply to protect what had already been promised to them. From people like Billy's grandfather and mother.

Nowadays the gold and silver in the Black Hills had mostly played out, but his father remained quite the adept miner. Wielding fear like a pick axe, he shoveled piety onto his parishioners' shoulders until they yielded. He pulled precious ore from their pockets and purses. They placed it right there in the pan for him and everything. All for the promise of an afterlife he couldn't guarantee.

His father wasn't a hypocrite in his own belief. Least not as far as Billy could tell. The man truly did believe in the salvation he sold. Problem was, that was all he believed in. So much so he forgot the importance of life here on earth.

Billy wasn't sure what he believed in. Religion and gods. Both his father's and those from his mother's people. They all seemed like myths. At least they did until the night of his sixteenth.

The night he met the devil.

She came to him in a curl of smoke rising from a rectangle of aluminum foil. She snaked her way up through the cheap plastic hull of a disassembled pen, slithered down his throat, and unfurled in the bowels of his lungs.

Billy did not recognize the devil, though she knew him well. For there had been a time when he nursed at her breast. But the evil one hid the truth back then.

His real mother had already left, her soul dealt away to a greasy-haired chemist, named Mel, but the terms of the transaction, bound the devil to linger and play nursemaid to a half-breed boy from Pierre. Bound to linger still.

Why? Why Why?

That's a question his father would've asked had he known. But even as much a Godly man as he considered himself, he failed to see the devil standing right before his eyes. Maybe because he was transfixed on the mansion and the golden streets waiting on him in eternity. For that, Billy would never forgive him. He didn't care how much talk he heard about Jesus and how he had died "so our sins could be forgiven."

Billy never met Jesus, but he'd sure heard plenty about his so-called savior. His dad had been flinging the name down from the pulpit, for as long as Billy could remember. At home Jesus took a backseat to his father's thunder about God Almighty, though his dad claimed they were one and the same. With a dose of the Holy Ghost to flesh out the recipe.

The recipe that created the crystals smoking on the foil was a hell of a lot more tangible, and Billy was all too ready to surrender to its power, on that night.

There in the Church of God basement, in the aptly name "Recreation Room," where wedding and funeral receptions alike had been held his whole life, where holidays were celebrated with potluck dinners of hashbrown casserole and sticky-sweet baked beans, in the corner behind the stacks of dusty hymnals, draped with plastic, checkerboard tablecloths, Billy huddled up with his two best friends, Jack Howard and Logan Two Elk, on the bench of an abandoned, out of tune spinet piano.

The meth belonged to Jack, who'd scored it from his older brother, who'd bought it from a guy who cooked the stuff up on the outskirts of town. The trio had smoked weed together plenty of times, but for whatever reason marijuana didn't get Billy high like it did his friends. He wanted that escape, craved it even. Anything to step away from the swirl of crap inside his head, but joints, the bong, even the medicinal candies never did it for him. Still he smoked with his friends, because it seemed like the thing to do. Last time though, his dad smelled it on him after, and the Godly thunder had rumbled for weeks.

Jack swore his dad wouldn't smell a thing this time, and that this stuff was guaranteed to get Billy high on a whole new level. Jack had smoked meth before, but Billy and Logan had never tried it. So Jack showed them how to hold the tube from the pen between their lips, while heating the crystals on the foil. "Chasing the dragon," he called it, and he made it look easy. But when Logan tried, he burned his finger and dropped the foil, and Jack called him a fucking moron for wasting some of the crystals.

Still they laughed and passed around the flask of whiskey Logan had sneaked out of his old man's cabinet that morning, while Jack folded another piece of foil so Billy could give it a try. Not taking any chances with the crystals, Jack held the lighter and the foil for Billy. When the smoke began to curl upward, he said, "Hit it, Birthday Boy."

Billy drew the small rising cloud of smoke deep into his lungs. And the devil came in with it.

The prickling twinge of pain crept through his airways. Sharp fingernails walked his flesh, conjuring memories of the time they tested his skin to test for allergies, only this time the needles were all inside him. The smoke burned and tingled its way down, like a hot whisper, until it settled in his chest. And his every nerve went cold, like the January wind.

Jack and Logan were cutting up and rambling on about how high they were, but Billy didn't feel any kind of euphoria. He held the smoke in, until his eyes rolled back in his head.

Hoping. Waiting.

Until he slowly began to exhale, and even in that dimly lit basement, it seemed as though he belched back six times the smoke he'd inhaled. A thick cloud escaped his lungs, and Billy's vocal cords vibrated and hummed, growing louder, picking up consonants and vowels until he cantered in a tongue none of them had ever heard.

It damn sure didn't sound like the moaning, Pentecostal ramblings his Dad's congregations fell into, when overcome by "The Spirit." No, there in that Church of God basement, the devil delivered a sermon meant only for Billy's soul to feel.

"What the fuck?"

Jack and Logan stared at him, in shock and disbelief. Which one had spoken, Billy couldn't discern. His ears were mostly filled with a demonic discourse solely he could hear. His body trembled and shook. He clenched his jaw and tensed the muscles in his legs and chest and arms, trying to make himself be still, but the tremors only grew stronger, until he give in to their power.

"What the fuck, Jack!" Logan ran his fingers through his long, black hair. "You said this shit was legit!"

This was all wrong. Billy knew that much. He stared at his friends, his wild eyes begging for help. He couldn't make his tongue work to form words the other boys would understand. He wanted to hush the sounds spewing from him and speak—to ask his friends what was going on—but they seemed so far away, and though their voices rang abnormally loud, their words were unintelligible.

"I don't know!"

"He only took one hit man. My brother gets spun on this shit all the time, and I've never seen him like this!"

"He's freaking out man!"

"Billy, Billy, Billy!"

His heart hammered his chest. Billy felt each individual bead of perspiration on his forehead, as the dull heat of Satan's grip settled in his gut. He itched to wipe the sweat away, but he couldn't lift his arm, bend his elbow, maneuver his wrist, or move his fingers. He could no longer distinguish where his body began, or ended, or if he even had a body still.

The air grew colder.

His belly hotter.

The room darker.

Blackness crept in on him, like a narrowing hallway, until that's all there was. And then from the depths of the maddening darkness, the lights grew bright. Jack was gone, Logan as well. Billy was alone, in a vast empty space. He wondered if he had died.

The sermon in his ears gave way to a pulsating buzz. His heartbeat maybe? No more like waves of energy filling his ears, like the electrical transformers on top of power poles, just before they blew. The light grew, until the vivid glare singed his eyes, though darkness still made up his periphery.

Billy feared he would never see again. Blinded, scared, and alone, he felt the wind first. Cool, moist, and unexpected. Then words carried by the wind ... *C'incá. C'incá. C'incá.*

Billy didn't know many Lakota words, but he knew this one. How? How did he know this word?

C'incá. C'incá. C'incá.

He remembered. There had been a time when Billy was younger, that he dreamed of his mother every night. In those dreams, she always used this word c'incá. Here, under this flood of light, he recalled those dreams as vividly as if they'd come the night before.

C'incá. C'incá. C'incá.

Billy did not remember his mother. Not the real her. She died and left him. His first tangible memory of her was in her casket. Though he wasn't even sure if that was a real memory, or one gained from a picture he found tucked in his dad's bible. He'd stolen the picture and burned it over in an empty lot, because he hated the idea of his dad quoting resurrection from a bible that held a picture of his lifeless mother.

He knew he had been young, when she died, maybe just a baby. A car wreck his dad always claimed, but that was a lie Billy snaked out even as a child. He had asked his father how she died so often that his father finally lost control and slapped Billy across the head. The only time his dad had ever struck him, but that smack stuck to Billy and convinced him of the wrongness behind the answer he'd been given. It also convinced him to stop asking.

Now, here in this place, the weight of that lifelong lie felt heavier than ever before.

C'incá. Her voice called on the wind. She was close. He felt her presence in the very reverberation of the word, but still he could see nothing against this glare. Billy reached forward hoping to touch her and the light moved around his hand, like the fog moves above a pond on a cold winter's morning.

But this was not fog. It was smoke. Cold, thick smoke. Billy cocked his head, unsure how smoke could be made cold. But now his nose was full of the smell of it. Sulphur and something else. What was it? He knew the scent, but his mind could not claim it.

C'incá.

Blood. That was the other smell.

Sulphur and blood, and still she called to him *C'incá. C'incá. C'incá.*

The stink of the blood took Billy back to one of the visits with his grandfather, when he was much younger. They'd gone to the reservation for Billy to witness something important. Billy stood and watched them cut into the belly of a buffalo. This smoke smelled much like that day. But both then and now, Billy had not fully grasped what he was supposed to take away from the experience.

Billy had understood that standing there, he had not felt like a half-breed, and now in this place, Billy didn't think it mattered at all what he was. Somehow, he understood it only mattered what he would be.

The smoke moved around him, and the glare of the light softened. He listened, but no longer did his mother's voice float in the air. Billy blinked again, and he spotted a shape ahead. The smoke flowed like water toward the shadows and Billy floated with it, though his feet never left the ground. Pulled toward the outline ahead, he squinted trying to unblur the image.

The thing loomed in front of him now. A being, human-like in shape, yet decidedly more substantial in both size and aura.

The smoke grew turbulent, like a spring river.

Billy tried to stop the pull, the ever quickening gliding. Farther. Deeper. Descent. He wasn't floating, so much as dropping. He could not halt the fall, but just as his fear threatened to overwhelm him, a whisper in his ear told him he would land safely.

The blood had gone from a scent in his nose to a taste on his tongue. Iron. And pulled by the magnetic force of that looming dark being, the undulant buzzing in his head turned into a sinister hiss not unlike the sound of the rattlesnake he'd killed on the banks of the river last summer.

Then both the buzz and the hiss were gone. And the wind grew stronger. Billy felt the ground beneath his feet yet again, slick and wet like a dewy morning.

He looked down, but under him the moist feeling was not dew. The grass ran crimson with blood. Billy knew this place. He'd been here, on one of the trips with his Grandfather. But it hadn't looked like this. Greasy

Grass his mother's people called this sacred ground. His father's knew it as Little Bighorn.

A hand reached out from the darkness and took Billy's, bidding him to walk. The being he'd seen a moment ago led him forward. Tonight Billy walked the field at Greasy Grass, hand in hand with Death, and the carnage was fresh. Horses torn apart. Scalps peeled back. Blood and sulphur, and the cool smoke curled around the two of them. Here, the ethereal substance was truly a mist that left moisture dripping off the carcasses of the many who'd fallen upon this ground.

Death stopped, and Billy looked down at the face of a man with a torn, stained uniform, and greasy blond curls, drenched in the blood of the grass. The face he saw was not only printed in the history books Billy had seen, but was etched into the story of his people and this land. Billy stared at the body by his feet.

Last stand? Hardly. There was nothing standing here. Not for this man. His foolish pride stained the grass red. The beast beside Billy stretched out his arm and pointed a long finger. There, in the bloody hand of the General, was a small spot of shiny silver.

The hand gripping Billy squeezed harder, and a warrior appeared there in the mist, walking up beside them. Billy felt his heartbeat fall in perfect time with this blood-covered boy, not much older than himself. The warrior stopped and met Billy's stare for a measure of three before bending to snatch what Billy now recognized was a coin from the dead General's hand. Letting out a war cry that rang loud and pierced the sky, the young warrior stood and walked on. As he faded into the mist, Billy spun up and away from the battlefield with the bony black hand still clutching his own.

Billy was surrounded again by nothing but the darkness and the smoke. And in the moment of silence that followed, he finally met his mother.

She was beautiful. She was love. She was fragile. She was broken. She was all of these things at once. Her heartbeat matched his own, and in that intertwined rhythm, one last time, he heard the Lakota word for "my child" … *c'inċá*.

Billy bathed there in the calm gentle flow of his mother's soul. He saw her as a little girl on the reservation, in the arms of his grandfather. Both of them younger and happier, laughing and playing in the sun. She looked to the man, with a boundless joy and admiration only a daughter could know. And his grandfather held her with the love only a father can possess for his daughter.

Then Billy saw her mature into a young woman. He watched her smile at his own father, who looked much like the man Billy knew, except somehow both stronger and softer. Billy couldn't remember ever seeing the smile he now witnessed on his father's face.

His grandfather appeared again. The man's dark, powerful face turned angry, and the black eyes that had smiled on Billy so many times, turned to rage, cursing shame and disgrace on his daughter. His mother cried and turned her head. And Billy saw that his father had been right. They had turned her out. His mother walked away and took the hand of Billy's father. Tears streaked her young cheeks.

A white glare shone, and sparkled on the smoke around them with prismatic color. His mother reappeared, dressed in the traditional white and blue of a Lakota wedding dress. With a backdrop of stained glass, he watched her smile through the sadness in her eyes and say, "I do."

His father wore a suit Billy was pretty sure he still preached in. His mother and father looked at odds with each other, standing there in the very church his dad now pastored. No one, not even Billy or his father could tell by looking at her, but she held a secret. There in her belly, Billy felt and heard a heartbeat. His heartbeat.

The vision cracked apart, and Billy shouted with pain.

"Billy! What the fuck Billy? Billy!"

He heard Logan Two Elks calling him. But despite the hurt, Billy was not ready to leave this place. He could still see and feel his mother here, and he fought to stay. Then the boys were gone again, and he saw his mother's small frame swell rounder, and more perfect, as she returned to the reservation.

The old man stared at her belly and spewed more disappointment, anger, and rage. She wailed in tears as he shouted. "You have disgraced our name and cursed that child!" The words stung Billy's ears and pierced his mother's heart. His chest pulled tight, and his breath stifled.

Billy watched her flee her childhood home and hurry into a fast-rising smoke, only to reappear at a run-down house with rusted-out cars and trash scattered across the yard. Decrepit curtains, torn and threadbare, stained with nicotine and god knows what, hung in the windows. She knocked and entered. A man with greasy, blond curls framing a gaunt, haggard face handed her a baggie in exchange for a handful of money.

His mother left, and Billy could breathe again. Soon however, the man called her back. Over and over again she was drawn to him, smoothly gliding, pulled like a magnet. She paid each time for the crystals, until she had no money to bring. She followed him in, and Billy closed his eyes when they went to the bedroom. His mother held another baggie when they were done, and Billy felt his knees shake and vomit press into his throat.

His mother cried and shriveled, as she walked from the soiled bedroom to the kitchen. Billy struggled to draw a breath when she pulled a glass pipe from her pocket. A white hot flame, held by a bony hand stretched from the peripheral darkness to heat the end. She loaded the baggy's contents into the pipe and brought it to her mouth, inhaling through the pipe as the crystals evaporated into smoke, snaked up the clear, glass tube, and entered her lungs.

Her eyes rolled back, and she shuddered, as she pulled in the vapor, just as Billy had done with the foil earlier. But this time, Billy felt it all the way to his bones. Pain then numbness. His mother smiled as the poison filled her veins.

Billy couldn't be certain what was real, what was dream. He watched her turn toward the man with the greasy, blond curls. She reached for him, and the man smiled and laughed.

The harsh laughter rang against Billy's ears, clanging like hammer on steel. Time and again that cruel laugh erased the beauty from his mother's face, as Billy watched her reach for and embrace both Greasy Curls and his baggies. At last the laughter died and Greasy Curls simply shook his head. His mom begged until the man laughed again. His mother's belly grew, and still she begged from bended knee. She turned her head skyward, an act that only brought more maniacal laughter.

Darkness fell around them all. Billy heard his mother scream. He saw her laid out in front of him, skinny and frail but swelled in the middle, with the child inside her. And as she lay there wailing, her belly split from top to bottom like the tearing of a thin fabric, and there he was.

Billy met himself on his sixteenth birthday.

He saw his own entry into this world. But he did not come into the world squirming and screaming. Rather he entered, blue and slimy and silent, amidst the powerful smell of blood and sulfur, no breath in his lungs.

His mother bowed her head. Greasy Curls stopped laughing and Billy stopped breathing. The dual heartbeat he'd felt and heard earlier was now just one. The pounding thump in his own chest. Billy's infant body lay lifeless, and would not draw his first breath, until finally his mother lifted her head and nodded once.

Billy gasped, along with his infant self. His lungs filled with air, and Greasy Curls' eyes flashed. Now in him, Billy saw the towering, monstrous being he'd seen earlier, standing before his mother. The beast extended his arms and Billy's mother wailed. She pulled her baby close, but the beast put a long, bony finger to her lips and held out its hand to take the child. Only then did his mother hand him to the beast.

The being cradled the squalling infant and dismissed his mother with a wave of his bony black hand. It ran its finger down the newborn's cheek and turned away, leaving his mother behind.

His mother crumpled to the floor and faded into the smoke, as Billy was pulled, spinning the opposite direction.

"Son! Do you hear me?"

Billy tried to shut his eyes against the glare, but someone had his eyelids pried open.

"Son! Son! Son!"

Fatigue settled in his bones. He'd never been more tired in his life. Despite the voices calling to him, he closed his mind and fell into a deep, dreamless sleep.

He awoke to new, different voices, different from those he'd heard during his trip with the devil and different from the voices in the church basement.

He recognized one of these voices as that of his father. "Drugs then," he said.

"No sir," said a voice Billy had never heard before. "The bloodwork came back clean. No trace of drugs. Nothing abnormal in any way."

"A kid doesn't just pass out and start convulsing and shouting gibberish for no reason," his father insisted. "He was completely unresponsive for a good fifteen minutes!"

"We're not real sure what happened. His cell counts are normal and his blood work's clean. I will order a complete CT Scan and an MRI, but at this juncture we have no reasonable explanation for your son's episode."

Billy still felt tired all the way to his soul, so he closed his eyes and drifted back to sleep, hoping for one more minute with his mother. But she did not return to him.

Three days later they let him go home, with no medical explanation for what happened down in that basement. But Billy's dad was far from satisfied.

"I looked through your phone," he said before they'd even pulled away from the hospital.

Billy said nothing.

"I read the texts from your friends."

Billy stared ahead. Neither Logan nor Jack had visited him in the hospital. Only a handful of parishioners from the church.

"I know they were there with you. I know one of them called 911."

Billy didn't give a shit what his dad knew. So he said nothing.

"I know drugs were involved."

They stopped for a red light. "You don't know half as much as you think you do."

His dad backhanded him across the mouth. Billy looked back and smiled.

"You've disgraced us. Shamed us. I can't pastor a congregation that knows my son is some kind of drug addict."

"Tell them I had a car wreck."

His dad's eyes narrowed. "What's that supposed to mean?"

"It means Jesus will forgive you for lying."

"How dare you!" His dad growled and raised the

back of his hand again, but when Billy unwaveringly met his stare, the man brought his palm back down to the steering wheel and drove on, when the light turned green.

At home they didn't speak. Not that day nor the next. Billy didn't much speak to anybody, not even his friends. They asked the same questions as the doctors and his father, but Billy refused to offer any kind of explanation. He couldn't say what he didn't know, and he feared the consequences of revealing what he felt was the truth. So he kept his mouth shut and his head down.

Still his dad spoon-fed him that deity soup of the Father, the Son, and the Holy Ghost as if he suspected the long, dark walk his son had taken.

Real or imagined, Billy had no idea. But a month later, on the front porch of their home, when his dad announced they were moving to Louisiana, Billy heard his mother's voice whispering in the wind, and knew he would land just fine.

The Favor
by Dan Johnson

Billy was a quiet one, preacher's son,
Hair black as midnight,
Eyes like the moon.

Jenny was a sweet thing.
He swore she was an angel,
When he saw her in Sunday school.

Billy was the new guy, so shy,
Took her five weeks,
Just to get him to talk.

He'd moved to Louisiana,
With his daddy who was pastoring,
The Second Street Church of God.

True love falls hard.
Couldn't keep those two apart.
Lord Billy loved that girl.

They knew their folks would throw a fit,
So they ran away and got hitched,
The two of them against the world.

Forty miles out of town,
The summer sun was going down.
That tiny diamond sparkled on her hand.

Driving through the bayou,
Jenny said she liked the view.

They pulled off in a mangrove stand.

Billy wrapped his arm around her,
Took a walk down by the water,
Thinking 'bout that wedding night ahead.

They came up on a fishing shack,
Shotgun leaning on the back,
The Malveaux brothers in the moonshine shed.

They turned around and made some ground,
But the brothers tracked them down,
Stopped when they heard that shotgun cock.

The biggest one said tie him up,
We'll have our fun with her,
And then we'll feed her to the gators, make him
watch.

Billy looked down at his bride,
Saw the tears that poor girl cried,
Jenny started begging for their lives.

The Malveaux brothers closing in,
Evil with a black toothed grin,
Hellfire lust in their eyes.

Jenny turned to Billy,
Saw a look she'd never seen,
As he started saying something like a prayer.

Then he reached down in his pocket,
For a hammered coin of silver,
She watched him as he flipped it in the air.

As it spun into the sky,
Thunder rolled and angels cried,
Darkness poured like blood out on the swamp.

And there behind the Malveaux brothers,
Stood one who could be no other,
Took 'em by the hands and made 'em walk.

As they stepped into the water,
Lightning flashed, the gators got 'em,
Them brothers' screams were drowned in mud and
blood.

Then the darkness slipped away,
Like a dream just as you're waking,
Silence fell around them as they stood.

Jenny tried to hold it all together,
But she couldn't tell just whether,
She was more relieved or scared.

Rescued from the arms of evil,
By that sacrilegious savior,
Would her soul be damned or was it spared?

Jenny tried to find the words,
To ask so much of Billy,
'Til she turned and saw the look that was in his eyes.

And all he said was "Babe,
When the devil owes you a favor,
You damn sure don't ask why."

Hemingway

Inspired by the song "Hemingway" by Dan Johnson

John Rivero turned eighteen in paradise.

He marked the occasion alone. First at sea, where he watched the sun rise. Just John and his flyrod. The morning water lay flat and calm and the fish spooky. Still he managed to catch and release a few nice bonefish and one decent barracuda, before noon. He stayed out as long as he dared, returning the borrowed skiff to the dock that afternoon. There his now former boss gifted him with a bottle of bourbon.

John did not care for whiskey. He preferred rum, but he appreciated the sentiment of the card which read, *Welcome to manhood. Best of luck, Captain Rick.* Captain Rick didn't give a damn it was illegal to gift an eighteen year old with a bottle of booze. Captain Rick was a man who created his own laws of right and wrong.

Hours later the bourbon sat openly on his dresser while he packed. John thought about cracking it open, but getting drunk would change nothing. So he left the bottle out, planning to drink it when he returned. If his dad didn't pour it out before then.

Given his dad's all-too-great care to never offend Captain Rick that seemed an unlikely scenario. His dad had worked for Captain Rick all of John's life. Captain Rick was somewhere close to seventy. Some two and a half decades older than his dad, but in John's eyes, the man understood him better than his own father ever had.

After turning out the lights, John lay on top of the covers and listened to his Lito's snores through the wall. His dad snored too, but tonight he remained awake, sipping from his own bottle. John knew this by the occasional tinkle of ice and scrape of the kitchen chair. John was grateful that he had not inherited the snoring traits of his father and grandfather. Such a habit would not go over well in basic training.

There had been no birthday present from his dad or Lito this year. Nor any going away presents. Not from his family anyway. His girlfriend had brought him rosary beads made from a dark pink coral. She told him her priest had blessed them. She also told him she'd blessed them, and that later she'd show him that blessing.

He would miss things from Key West. The cheers from back in the fall, when he scored all those touchdowns. The morning, noon, and night crows of the gypsy chickens. Captain Rick, and mornings out on the water.

John did not think he would miss Emily. Though that night, he fell asleep fondling the beads she'd given him.

He awoke the next morning to a text from Emily. A picture of the rosary hanging against her bare chest. Her nipples a perfect match to the color of the coral. The text read, *Stay safe for me and I will give you an even better kind of blessing when you come back.*

Eighteen and a day, John stood outside the apartment complex and took in the salty morning taste of paradise. He would not taste this air again anytime soon.

Paradise lost.

John was sick of hearing about paradise and he was especially sick of Milton's poem. Struggling through it in school had been bad enough, but these last few months, since John enlisted, his father had taken to reciting the piece aloud. Never before a religious man, he heaved plenty of hardcore Old Testament into Milton's famous words. John didn't take the bait.

He didn't believe any of that shit about man's disobedience unleashing death into the world, nor did he actually think of this place as paradise. Though, the word was hard to escape here on this island, where they printed paradise on all the travel brochures, and scrawled paradise in fancy script upon the postcards they sold along Duval Street and down at Mallory Square. They even painted the designation, "Paradise USA" on the Welcome to Key West sign.

They being the promoters, the hucksters, the island's dependents. They however, forgot one undeniable truth. Paradise belongs to nature. Mother superior in the truest state. In the case of Key West, she built paradise upon the carcasses of her children. And someday, she would reclaim their souls.

John Rivero did not fear that day. No resident of the Keys feared that kind of end. They feared hurricanes, government blockades, and environmental pollution because the tourists cared about such things, but no one pondered the coral detritus slowly rotting beneath their feet. Not the promoters, the hucksters, or the island's dependents. And certainly not the tourists captivated by Mother Nature's sultry seduction.

The coral skeletons that made up the very bones of this archipelago had long ago served their purpose and now lay forgotten, beneath the white sand and shallow turquoise waters.

Forgotten, like a dream unpursued.

John did not want to become his father. Stuck in one place, working for one man forever. Even after the dreams he once held were gone and forgotten. At eighteen, John Rivero still held hope there was more to life. Despite this gnawing hunch in his gut, he had no idea what this so-called "more" would look like. Not with the limited view of the world Key West offered. John had always been good at seeing things others could not. Like tailing bonefish and silent barracuda gliding through the water. But to spot them out on the water, he stood high on a platform. And he stayed focused, because there was no high ground in the Keys.

This morning, he didn't need a lofty perch to see the recruiter was late. So much for the stiff regiment of Army life his dad preached. John did not look back at the second story window, but he could feel his father and grandfather both up there watching.

Waiting.

They didn't have to wait long. John inhaled only a few more lungfuls of paradise before a white sedan, too shiny and free of rust to belong in this place, rounded the corner and stopped beside him. John settled in the passenger seat, but said nothing. He'd learned at an early age to keep his eyes open and his mouth shut. The habit made him a deadly hunter out on the water, but in the years before he came to live with his father in paradise, his silence had kept him safe. Therefore John equated silence with survival. For both the prey, and the predator.

John felt like both as he rode across the island.

An eddy of thoughts swirled through him. As always, the what ifs sung to him like the sirens of Greek mythology he'd read about. John tried to fight the urges and keep them inside his head, but he rarely succeeded. What if the fishing is better around the next cay? What if the story proved more exciting in the next book? What if the next girl to smile his way was softer, and firmer, and something more than the last?

But not his father. He stuck only to proven waters. Read only the classics. And far as John knew, had known only the one woman who'd broken his heart and disappointed him so.

John Rivero lived for his next, next. But trapped in paradise, on this island built upon dead coral, at the farthest southern tip US 1, John Rivero had run completely out of nexts.

The Army promised to fill that void.

The recruiter drove him to the airport because his father refused. At the terminal, John and the man shook hands. The recruiter said, "Keep those eyes sharp. I need you to take me out when you get back. Still chasing that trophy bone."

John smiled. The man would never catch a trophy. He'd guided the recruiter countless times and put him on many a big fish, but the man was too slow, too tentative with a fly rod in his hands. The recruiter hooked a large Tarpon once, but John was the only big catch the man had ever landed.

After going through security, John tucked the rosary back inside his shirt and sat silent, away from others so he could look at the picture from Emily. He wondered if she would go to confession for this sin. He hoped not. John wanted to think the picture existed in secret, only between the two of them.

John often teased her about going to confession and about her fondness for invoking the name of patron saints for everything she did. But part of him envied her faith. John didn't hold such trust. Not even for the things he could see and touch.

When they began boarding he wrote Emily a quick text. *Thx for the send off and the blessings. Love the pic. Pls send one of your smile too. Every soldier needs a pretty girl to stare at when he gets homesick.* He felt stupid and sappy, but hit send anyway. At least someone cared he was leaving.

Nervous because he'd never flown anywhere, he turned his phone off and took a seat. When the flight lifted from the runway, John leaned awkwardly down to stare out the small window. He easily picked out their apartment building and wondered if his dad and Lito were still standing there in the window, watching.

Waiting.

The plane banked and headed out over the turquoise waters John knew so well. Beneath a cloudless blue sky, John continued to stare as they turned north and crossed over the Everglades. He looked off to the east toward Homestead and Miami, but he couldn't make out much in the humid haze. His mom was out there somewhere. No doubt living with yet another loser. Unless she happened to be back in jail.

The plane touched down soon enough and the flight attendant announced, "Welcome to Georgia."

John smiled happy she hadn't said welcome to paradise. He scrambled to make his next flight, but still managed to grab a window seat. This second leg took him to St Louis where he was disappointed to discover the famous arch did not actually span the girth of the Mississippi River. The so-called Gateway to the West didn't look like much from the plane, but his journey west was nearly over anyway. One more short flight and he would land at his next home, Fort Leonard Wood, Missouri.

With an hour before that flight, he powered up his phone and discovered a new picture of Emily, smiling with her auburn eyes and those soft, full-lips. Maybe he would miss her a little.

A bus took him to the base and there, he finally found the regimented routine his dad warned him of. But John was ready for it. He listened well. He knew how to follow orders. They first learned how to respond with "Yes, drill sergeant!" to any and every order given. And then John was instructed to do something he could not, would not do.

"Call home and say three sentences!" the drill sergeant barked. "I have arrived at Fort Leonard Wood. I
am safe. I will call you when I can." The man stared hard
at his new charges. "Say no less! Say no more!"

The words meant nothing to John. He could speak
them. What he could not do, was call home. He would
not give his dad the satisfaction. And Emily would expect more. She would be distraught when he did not
deliver on that need, so John could not call her. Instead
he dialed Captain Rick, and spoke the words. "I have
arrived at Fort Leonard Wood. I am safe. I will call you
when I can." He hung up without waiting a reply.

His dad was right about one thing. The Army killed
John Rivero.

They sweated away the John first. Under that muggy
Missouri sun, no one called him John. Only Rivero. And
Rivero excelled where others struggled. His days carrying the football for the Key West Conchs and poling
Captain Rick's boats helped prepare him for the physi-
cality of it all. The patience and steady hand required to
stalk fish out on the flats had honed his hunting skills.
And his dad's discipline and constant disapproval both
weighed far more than the pressure from his drill sergeant. Then again, Private Rivero did not disappoint his
drill sergeant nearly as often.

Rivero did not notice when John died. While he
settled into the routines of basic training, his first name
rotted away and settled beneath his feet like Mother Nature's coral. The instructors steadily reminded him, his
next would come soon enough.

In those earliest days of basic, Private Rivero wrote

letters to his dad and to Lito. Letters that went unan-
swered. He also wrote his maternal grandmother in
Homestead, and eventually got a letter back saying she
was proud of him, that her father had served in Korea,
and that yes, his mother was back in jail. After a few
weeks of fondling her coral beads each night, Rivero
wrote Emily, who wrote back three letters to his one.

He penned one letter to Captain Rick. He meant
it as an explanation for what had to have been an odd
and unexpected phone call. For whatever reason, Rivero
dumped more into that letter than the others. He wrote
about his fear, his hopes, his day-to-day routine. He
wrote Captain Rick the unfettered truth of the things
trapped in his mind. Afterward, he felt better.

Captain Rick wrote back one simple paragraph
scribbled on the back of the same postcards he mailed
to clients.

Hello Boy,

> *Your old man can be a prick. So can the
> rest of the world. Don't let any of 'em grind
> you down. Be your own fucking man.*

> *Captain Rick*

Rivero saved the card even though he'd been looking at the picture of his old boss standing with a five
hundred pound marlin all his life. No one had ever ac-
cused Captain Rick of humility, so the image graced the
brochures, the postcards, every last letterhead. It even

covered the door of the small office at the marina. In it, he wasn't smiling.

Captain Rick never smiled. He shared that trait with John Rivero senior. Though Rivero's father had hard, dark eyes, whereas Captain Rick looked at the world through soft, gray-blue eyes the color of a steel gaff hook. In those eyes, a touch of mirth. Especially when the captain had been drinking.

Between the running, crawling, climbing, and training, Private Rivero wrote. Not only letters to others, but notes for himself. His first purchase at the PX, beyond the necessary hygiene items, was a leather-bound journal. He'd never been a writer before, but without the escape of time on the water, pen and ink seemed the only outlet for the thoughts trapped inside his head.

When he had nothing to write, he read Emily's letters, but her declarations of unwavering love unnerved him. She wanted to come to his graduation ceremony for basic training, but her parents refused to help her get to Missouri. In truth Rivero was glad, though he pretended otherwise.

By the time AIT rolled around, Rivero had a steady habit of reading, writing, and regaling the other guys with tales from paradise. He told them fishing stories, and tales of girls in bikinis, and spun thrillers about hurricanes that never were. The guys didn't care much about the truth, so long as his stories entertained.

These were the habits that penned the final chapter of John Rivero.

The tale of how he came to be nicknamed Hemingway is no great mystery. A tough swaggering kid from

Key West? With a flair for writing and love of adventure? And the patience to sit quietly over a good book, yet held the charisma to hold an audience with a bawdy tale? The name Rivero still appeared on his uniform, but by the time he finished training and joined his unit, Hemingway wore his new moniker as if it were Kevlar. Impervious to his past, Hemingway was the death of a boy named John, and the birth of an American soldier soon bound for a foreign land.

Hemingway was an asshole.

So wrote Captain Rick in reply to the mention of the nickname, but the declaration did not feel like a condemnation so much as an observance. Key West rumor claimed Captain Rick had been a smuggler during and after the Cuban revolution. Maybe he'd known Hemingway. Maybe not. The Captain would brag about fishing and women and his ability to outdrink any man north of the Marquesas, but he did not talk about Cuba. Never.

Gun, drugs, cigars, refugees. The rumors and stories varied, but no one dared mention such a thing in the man's presence. No one ever challenged Captain Rick on a damn thing.

For the first time. John 'Hemingway' Rivero wondered why.

He turned the theories over in his head without ever finding a solid answer.

When it came time to deploy, Hemingway felt like the rainwater gushing from a downspout back home. With every unlived moment, every unsaid word, every untaken step dumped from the sky, rolled over a rooftop and spraying through the narrowed hole of his immediate future. He couldn't do a lot to change any of those things. Not until he got back. But he could write to Captain Rick. Man-to-man and ask the things even his father did not have the guts to bring up. So he did, but no letter, not even a postcard came back. Not from Captain Rick.

Both before and after deployment, the occasional letter drifted in from his maternal grandmother in Homestead. *She prayed for him every night. His cousin Byron had signed to play ball at Alabama. His mother had been released to a rehab facility.*

Only Emily's letters came from paradise. Hemingway rarely wrote back. His training had made one thing clear. Eyes forward. Focus. Not on the past. Not on what was behind you, but rather on what might be ahead. All of his life he'd been waiting for someone to validate that philosophy.

Besides, even the original Hemingway left a girl behind in Key West. He took off for Havana and never looked back. Twentysome-odd years later, a horde of young teenagers fled Communist Cuba under Operation Peter Pan. His Lito had been one of them, and not once had Rivero ever caught his grandfather staring wistfully to the south.

Two different men, in different times, both leaving one love behind in search of their next adventure. Now here was a third, ready to do the same. So Hemingway wrote one last letter to Emily. Plain and to the point, he told her to forget him and move on. Writing the letter felt good, but his gut ached after he dropped it in the mail. He wondered if the original Hemingway ever regretted the woman he left behind.

Then again, a mere ninety miles separated Key West from Cuba, so his predecessor had been free to change his mind had he desired.

Eight thousand miles from both sides of paradise, in a dusty Army camp, in a place of rock and dirt and rubble, of browns and grays, of grit and sand—a young man they all called Hemingway held a fresh letter from Emily and wondered for the first time, if maybe he should've stayed back in Key West. If he should have made a different choice.

Off in the distance, the mountains held a touch of white and Hemingway often stared longingly at those frosted peaks. If paradise were to be found in this land, it had to be up there, where the earth rose to touch the sky of its own accord. His patrols never ranged so far. Stuck down below, where all-too-often the earth ruptured into dark smoky sky, Hemingway missed the blues and greens associated with paradise. He missed the smell of salt in the air, the taste of ocean spray on his lips, the lap of the waves against the hull of the boat. He missed paradise.

Yet the word taunted him even here, where like the native plants it grew in unlikely places to poke and scratch and grab hold of a man. *Another day in paradise. Paradise By The Dashboard Light.* The ubiquitous, *trouble in paradise* all tossed about like shrapnel from some fucking Haji's third-rate bomb.

They thought they were being funny.

They being the soldiers, the scared, the brave, the dependent on one another.

But they forget one undeniable truth. Paradise did

not belong to man.

They joked about the shitty weather, the sand-storms, the whacked-out primitive land they patrolled. They mocked their own fate as easily as they did the Haji's way of life.

Hemingway slept inside a CHU, Army speak for Containerized Housing Unit, five feet away from SPC Austin Bayless. Together they endured the wind, the sand, the twelve-hour patrols turned to seventy-two hour stints of sleep deprived hell. They talked long into the night, when one or both of them couldn't sleep. Bayless, in his slow Texas drawl, told Hemingway about the big bass back in Texas. Hogs, he called them, and Heming-way shared his own fish tales of hundred pound Tarpon. Bayless had a wife, a young son, and a nine month old baby girl back in what he called paradise—Waco, Texas.

Hemingway had only his coral rosary beads, and a girl he might or might not love. He had her letters too, but he only read one after he broke up with her. The others he stored unopened in a box beneath his bunk. Her name and handwriting were enough to make him all the more homesick. The last thing he needed was to read such sadness.

Bayless got letters and packages from home. And made phone calls that often left him red-eyed. Yet, he still greeted each morning with resolve.

He was one of them Groundhog Day fuckers that began every day the exact same way. Stretching his pale, freckled arms wide, he'd wink, if Hemingway had his eyes open, and proclaim, "Another day in Paradise."

In that singular moment Hemingway hated his

roommate. But he forgave him just as fast, because Bayless would add, "Rise and shine, Brother. We got huntin' to do."

Brothers.

Hemingway never had one until he got here. Now he claimed four. His team depended on him, and Hemingway on them. Even though they too enjoyed firing that single word upon him. Here, among these men, his brothers, any and every weakness was exposed to the harsh elements as both a test and testament. So when Sergeant Sanchez sang "Paradise By The Dashboard Light" by the soft glow of the navigation system, Hemingway joined in and sang along. And when Pfc. Jennings shouted, "We got trouble in Paradise!" Hemingway hunkered down and readied the big fifty not with irritation, but fierce determination to fight for, and with his brothers.

Paradise?

Yeah, it was a real place you could find on the map, but Hemingway had learned from his brothers everyone held a different map.

He also learned to be careful about revealing what got under your skin.

From Key West to Waco to Sgt. Sanchez's San Diego and Jenning's Rocky Mountains, they each held a place they were fighting to return to. Except 1st Lt. Ware. As team leader, 1st Lt. Ware led them everywhere, but the man didn't seem to have a compass of his own. No place he longed to return. The son of a general, he'd grown up on military bases the world over. Twice divorced before his thirtieth birthday, Lt. Ware said he'd worry about finding paradise in his next life because this one belonged to the US Army and the two women to whom he already paid alimony.

Hemingway hated the night patrols most. By day his eyes were as trusted as any piece of equipment in the regiment. Turned out spotting the odd anomaly along a dusty roadside wasn't much different than spotting a tailing bonefish among turquoise waves. The recruiter had been right about that. Even if he couldn't handle a flyrod.

By day or night they rolled along at the blistering pace of four miles per hour. Hemingway shared stories from paradise. He told them about the time a hot granddaughter of an Alabama senator blew him in the back room while her bloated granddaddy smoked illegal Cuban cigars on the other side of the wall. He told them about the dumbass from Omaha who got half his cock mangled by a Black Tip when he wouldn't listen how to hold the damn shark before he posed for a picture. And he told them he was going to start his own guide service when he got out.

A fact he hadn't even known himself until he spoke the words out loud.

Captain Rick would understand. His dad would not. Fuck his dad.

His brothers listened to both the stories and the dream. They promised to come down and go fishing once they all got out.

Fellow Pfc. Jennings called Denver home. He too flyfished, so in return Hemingway promised to come visit Colorado's narrow streams at first chance. Jennings was a short stocky guy of twenty-five. Part Chia pet, you could damn near watch the dark whiskers grow from his cheeks.

The bond of men trapped together in that RG-31 grew much the same way. Explosions, RPG attacks, random fire, and at times, their own short tempers, all hacked away at who they'd once been. And yet each day, the team grew together into what each of them would eventually be.

Thicker. Stronger. Unyielding brothers.

They all told their share of stories, but rarely did they get much out of Lt. Ware while on route clearance. Beyond the wire he was demanding and stoic and completely A.J., but back at the Forward Operating Base, in the sanctity of his or others' CHU, he'd go on a rant about the chain of command. Those rants always led to a story about his dad, and how fucked up it had been to grow up in perpetual basic training.

Eventually Hemingway broke down and told them about his dad. The guys especially enjoyed the impersonation of his dad reading Milton's *Paradise Lost* with Old Testament fervor. Soon enough they procured their own copies and often broke out in memorized sermon.

They were perhaps the only team of soldiers in the world that could recite seventeenth century poetry while searching out bombs stashed by angry insurgents.

> *To mortal men, he with his horrid crew*
> *Lay vanquisht, rowling in the fiery Gulfe*
> *Confounded though immortal: But his doom*
> *Reserv'd him to more wrath; for now the thought*
> *Both of lost happiness and lasting pain*

This mockery lifted Hemingway. That they would take the time and effort to read and learn such passages revealed a level of devotion he'd never been part of. And soon enough, Milton's words became not a source of anguish, but joy in his memories.

They also teased him about Emily when they caught him looking at her picture. The one of her face, not the blessing of the beads. That one Hemingway kept to himself, because even among brothers, some things are sacred. He didn't tell them he'd broken her heart.

There in the cramped space of that RG-31, surrounded by the smell of sweat and beef jerky and Sanchez's cinnamon Dentyne gum, dirt and dust filtered through their nostrils. The rattle of equipment and the hum of the engine filled their days or nights, depending on the mission. Decked in full battle rattle, they kept supply routes clear, made special runs to ensure roads were safe for visiting dignitaries, and they cleared the way for emergency operations.

Either way, they slow-rolled mile after mile of dangerous, shitty roads, while to their rear, other soldiers, on other missions, chugged along behind, cursing the tedious speed but grateful someone else cleared the way.

Third trip outside the wire.

That's how long Hemingway went before he experienced his first IED. The smell is what he most remembered afterward. That, and the sound of dirt raining down atop metal. No one got hurt that day, but they were lucky. Rigged for remote detonation, the cocksucker got antsy and shot his wad early. They'd just started down a little gully when it went off four, maybe five foot in front of the RG.

Later in bed, after Bayless had begun to breathe steady and heavy, Hemingway took out the rosary. He didn't know the words Catholics said in prayer, but he silently voiced his own oath. One for all fifty-five beads. His promises simple. Let him make it back, and he would never again leave paradise. Let him make it back, and he would make everything up to Emily. Let him make it back, and he too would seek God.

A week later another IED blew directly beneath them. Fucking thing went off with enough force to rock the RG onto its side. The explosion knocked Sanchez straight the fuck out.

Hemingway puked. Not when it went off, or even right after, but all that night and into the next day. They were supposed to have the day off, but then a supply line had to shift to another route and they got called out.

Their RG was out of commission and Sanchez was off patrol with a concussion so Lt. Ware took his navigation duty, leaving them a man short. On the next run, Hemingway got shifted around and for the first time found himself up in an open turret. There he discovered his gift.

Searching the road for any and every disruption, like scanning the waves for the tip of the tail on a feeding bonefish. Gray ghosts of another kind.

He spotted the devil's seeds with unprecedented accuracy. He not only saw them, he felt them in the very marrow of his bones. He couldn't explain it, but when a bomb was nearby he felt a buzz, a vibration that the others dubbed his Spidey Sense when he tried to explain.

Remote detonation. Pressure plates. Wired.

Hemingway felt them all.

Hemingway found them all.

The months slipped by in this manner.

The letter arrived the day before his birthday, with John Rivero Jr. scrawled in his dad's rough hand. No one else ever included the Jr. part. The envelope did not look like a birthday card, but Hemingway didn't care to open it and find out for sure.

Fuck his dad.

Six months and twenty-one days into deployment, Hemingway was no longer that same boy. He sought roadside bombs, not the approval of his father.

He'd seen real shit go down. He'd eaten breakfast with soldiers that never came back to eat lunch. He'd witnessed men lose everything from their mind, to their legs. He'd survived his third, fourth, and fifth IEDs. He'd lain awake for hours wondering why some escaped whole, and others did not. He'd pondered the minds of those who spent their days building bombs to bury in the dirt, not knowing, or even caring, who'd find the damn thing. He'd seen women and kids and goats mangled and burnt and blown apart, because they'd stepped in the wrong fucking place.

He wrote logs in his journal questioning what in this godforsaken place was worth fighting for, while some-where some fat bastard sat behind a desk deciding it was worth billions of dollars and thousands of lives to come to this fucking place and assert military might. And for what? Hemingway had no fucking idea.

Because a handful of assholes hijacked those damn planes? Because Americans feared it could happen again? Or because fighting a goddamn war fed a whole bunch of cake eaters?

All these boots in the sand wouldn't rebuild those towers. Nor did it mean another sick fuck wouldn't slip through the cracks. He came to realize—evil people find ways to do evil shit. And often as not, their weapon was a pen, not a gun.

Paradise?

If every map had a different red X, Hemingway had no doubt this hellhole marked the spot for some defense contractor CEO, but you could bet your ass the motherfucker never planned a personal visit.

The word motherfucker brought his thoughts back to the letter. He stared at his Dad's handwriting. A motherfucker in every sense of the word. Sliding his thumb under the corner flap Hemingway tore open the envelope.

Stuffed inside, a newspaper clipping, and nothing else.

No letter.

No card.

With shaking hands he couldn't explain, Hemingway pulled the clipping from the envelope. He turned it over. Emily smiled up at him.

Mr. and Mrs. Roger Atwell of Key West
announce the engagement and forthcoming
wedding of their daughter Emily Atwell
to Caleb Pendleton, also of Key West. The

wedding will ...

His heart pounded and his mouth turned dry.

He finished reading, but his body went cold.

He tried to remember when he'd last gotten a letter from her. He dropped to his knees and pulled out the box with her unopened letters. The most recent on top. Postmarked just over three months ago. He ripped it open and scanned the words.

> *Miss you ...*
> *Wish you'd write back ...*
> *I don't understand why ...*

Not one damn word about her getting married. Hemingway's phone didn't work here. He kept it charged only to take pictures and look at the ones stored on his phone. But Bayless had a phone that worked. He called home all the time.

Where the fuck was Bayless?

Sergeant Sanchez found Hemingway before Hemingway found Bayless.

"Apache went down. They say the crew's banged up but alive. Route out that way is dirty. We gotta run clearance."

"Fuck me." Hemingway punched the makeshift latrine's corrugated tin wall.

"You all right?" Sanchez laid a hand on his shoulder.

He shrugged out of Sanchez's grip. "Just a bad fucking night. I needed to find Bayless."

"I sent him to gear up, so go grab your shit, and

you'll find him."

Bayless was holding the newspaper clipping when Hemingway walked in. He tossed it back on the bed and said, "Fuck her man."

Hemingway nodded once, and swallowed hard.

Twenty minutes later they were outside the wire eating dust with a long convoy of ass behind them in case shit went down out there in the dark.

This ground had been swept and monitored so they made good time for the first few miles. Up in the turret, Hemingway clenched his jaws and jacked with his night vision. Constant radio chatter droned on, but he didn't pay much attention.

So he hadn't written her back since he'd been here? Still, she didn't have to go and marry that pansy-ass, preppy little prick, Caleb! Her parents finally got what their wish—for Emily to ditch him and marry a rich, white bread kid.

The thoughts stayed embedded in his mind, but when the RG slowed, he knew they were closing in on dirty road. Here, he couldn't afford to be distracted, so to exorcise the demons he reached inside his collar and gave a good hard yank. The beads had hung there all these months, but they snapped easily enough. A few pieces of coral tinkled down into the RG. He pitched the rest to the side of that dark gravel roadway.

Liberated, he focused on the road ahead.

A couple hours later they pulled up on the crash site. Despite the array of weaponry, or perhaps because of it, they arrived without incident.

The crew in the Apache had sat their bird down

hard, so the crew had multiple injuries. Hemingway's team made a broad sweep to clear ground for the medevac before setting up position as part of the perimeter guard.

At midnight, he turned nineteen there in BFE. Watching.

Waiting.

But Haji never came to the party, so the sun broke the horizon with the team still sitting there, pulling another dull, uneventful mission of guard duty. Afternoon arrived before they finally started back the way they'd come.

Hungry, tired, and still eager to make that phone call, Hemingway watched the roadside for the rosary. He wished he'd taken note of where he'd flung them, but everything looked pretty much the same even by day. And last night, he hadn't been thinking clearly.

He didn't regret tossing the rosary, but still he wanted one last look at them lying in the dust. That seemed a fitting end to him and Emily.

He never spotted them.

Neither did he see the IED.

Smoke.

Thick and cloying.

Screaming.

The acrid stench of the former barely registered, before the latter broke through the thrum inside his skull. Still he did not understand. Where he was, or what had happened.

The screams.

Penetrating, unrelenting screams.

He tried to yell shut the fuck up at whoever was screaming, but a gagging cough choked off his words.

Silence.

Only then did he realize the screams had been his own.

It was so fucking dark. Hemingway tried to reach up and rub his eyes. They were full of sand or dirt or something, but when he tried to move he couldn't. His arm was pinned. His body too.

More shouts came now.

Shouts from all around.

Hemingway groaned, but not loud enough to match Lt. Ware's commands. "Bayless! Bayless! God Damn it Bayless, you fucking answer me!"

Hemingway gathered his strength and lurched once hoping to free his body, but pain exploded and then his world shrank away to nothing.

He left his blood, his soul, and one eye there in that land of dust and dirt and rubble. On that same rocky road that claimed Emily's coral rosary.

His legs he left in Germany. Or so they told him. It would be months before Hemingway began to remember much of anything.

Eventually, he landed back in the States, at an Army hospital down in Texas. Not all that far from Waco, where they'd buried Spc. Austin Bayless.

Hemingway missed the funeral. He didn't make Sanchez's either. He'd been in a coma in Germany for both.

In theory, he could've made Emily's wedding to that asshole down in the Keys. Except he was busy in Texas at the time. Learning to walk again.

They gave him stubbies first. Short little temporary prosthetics that looked more like a seat stand for a boat than a leg. On them, he learned how to hobble like some kind of GI Joe mini me.

He turned twenty between surgeries. Then twenty-one in rehab.

Still more months passed before he got his new permanent legs. Carbon fiber in flat back with real working knees and sculpted feet for his shiny new Nike's.

Eleven surgeries, and better than two years after that IED explosion, Hemingway made it back to Florida where no one called him by that nickname, which was just as well since he no longer liked to tell stories.

John Rivero went to live with his mother in Homestead, because that seemed the best of a slew of bad options. His dad had come to Germany, and again to Texas, but they didn't have much to say to each other. The I-told-you-so in his dad's eyes spoke loud enough for both of them.

One month turned into two. Then three and four. He hated Homestead.

Cousins. The nosy next door neighbor. The gnarled old bastard his mom was banging. They all picked and prodded and hinted around the questions. They wanted to hear about that day, but none of them had the guts to come out and ask for the tale of how he nearly died.

The rehab. The counseling. The life skill training. He grew sick of it all. Restless at being tied down to this place, he longed to escape. To take care of the business that haunted him in his sleep, the lives of the brothers he was responsible for.

His dad called a few times. Told him he could come home, but when John's reply came in Old Testament fervor ...

Of Man's first disobedience, and the fruit
Of that forbidden tree whose mortal taste
Brought death into the World, and all our woe,

... his dad only hung up.

John thought he'd severed all ties to paradise, but then two old buddies from his football team drove up. They weren't so delicate as everyone else.

"Man, what happened over there? Tell us how it went down. What was it like when it went off?"

John made up a bullshit story. Was easier that way. He told them they were under fire from Taliban on one side and al-Qaeda on the other. He told them it wasn't an IED at all, but a shoulder-fired missile stolen from the Soviet Union. They bought every fucking word. He could've told them it had been Mussolini or the Viet Cong, because they hadn't been there. Because what they knew about life and death came from pixels on a TV.

But really he lied, because the truth was too fucking painful. Two men died, two of his brothers, because he'd been more focused on fucking rosary beads than IEDs.

Captain Rick came too. That was the strangest visit of them all. John called out "Come in!" at the knock on the door. He didn't have his prosthetics on, and his mom was back in the kitchen.

His old boss stepped inside, but never made it past the doorway. He stared at the floor where John's feet should have been.

"Goddamn it," he said.

His mom walked in about then, and it had never dawned on John the two would know each other, though it was obvious they did. They didn't speak for an awkward count of fifteen, maybe twenty. Then his mom said, "Hello Rick."

Not Captain Rick, but just plain old Rick.

John had never heard anyone omit the word Captain when speaking to him.

Silence hung between them until his mom walked right passed Captain Rick, and on out the front door. He rushed after her, and John could hear their raised voices out in the yard, but he didn't go to the effort of moving closer so he could overhear more. Whatever they had to say to one another was none of his business.

After a bit, Captain Rick came back in looking every bit of his nearly seventy-five years. "The world is a fucked up place kid. I'm sorry for what they did to you. You need or want a job, come see me. I'll rig up a boat for you."

John nodded to keep from speaking. He wasn't sure he trusted his emotions, and Captain Rick was not a man you shed tears in front of.

"I should've wrote back. Told you about Cuba when you asked."

John shook his head. "I don't much give a fuck about Cuba."

"No. You got your own personal hell to dwell on. That's what Cuba was, still is for me. I damn near died there. Like you damn near died over there. I guess I was lucky, but that sounds like a shitty thing to say now that I've said it."

John nodded. "That's what all the doctors and nurses and rehab therapist say. "You're lucky to be alive."

Captain Rick ran a thick hand through his whiskers. "I don't imagine you feel very damn lucky."

"Nope."

"Neither do I," Captain Rick said. "Maybe there's no such thing as luck."

The clock on the wall ticked and Captain Rick stared at it a minute before saying, "I never could stand to listen to the goddamn ticking of a clock."

"I can't hear it," John said. "Too much ringing inside my head."

"My ears used to ring when I boxed. Back in Cuba. I was good, but only because I could take a punch. I outlasted better boxers that didn't know what to do when I took their best shot." Captain Rick pulled something out of his pocket. He turned the object over a few times studying both sides before he pitched it in the air.

John caught it in his fist.

"That's what you gotta do now. The cocksuckers gave you their best shot. Now outlast 'em."

John opened his fist and stared down at an ancient silver piece. A coin, but it wasn't perfectly round like today's money. This coin had been made with human hands long ago. A face, mostly rubbed away, covered one side, and a big, long-legged eagle that gave off a strange, evil sort of vibe covered the flip side, along with a couple of foreign words.

"What is this?"

"Tyrian Shekel," Captain Rick said. "That asshole Hemingway gave it to me down in Cuba for winning a boxing match I shouldn't have won. He'd bet on me for some damn reason, and he left with more money from the fight than I did. The girl I'd been fucking. She left with him too, but I was too beat up to do her any good that night anyway. My ears rung like a motherfucker for weeks, but when I held that coin I somehow felt lucky."

The coin felt both hot and cold in John's hand, but he didn't feel any luckier than he had before Captain Rick pitched it to him.

"I hung onto it, and carried it with me all these years. Your mom asked me a long time ago to keep an eye on you. But hell, I didn't do a very good job. Maybe that coin will bring you more luck than it ever did me."

"Thought you said there wasn't any such thing as luck?"

"Shut up, Boy and put it in your pocket. Forget all about luck, and learn to trust your gut. It's about the only thing in this world that'll never lie to you.

John pocketed the coin.

Captain Rick asked, "People still calling you Hemingway?"

"Not many."

"Good. Tell your mother I said, goodbye."

After Captain Rick was gone, John pulled out the coin and stared at both sides for a good long time, but he didn't say a damn word to his mother. Not even when he caught her stealing his Percocet that afternoon. Instead, he left the next morning without a word to anyone. Because his gut told him to.

He strapped on his legs, stuck his Purple Heart in a duffel bag along with few changes of clothes, and took off in the modified Jeep the VA had helped him apply for.

For the first time since the explosion he felt a purpose, a calling, and with it came a tingle in his bones not unlike the one he'd once felt when an IED was near. He wore his old camouflage coat because now he was cold all the damn time. He blamed the metal legs for that, and a whole lot else.

Heading west, he was antsy and maybe a little scared. He'd not truly been on his own ever, and since the accident he'd only ever gone a few hours without someone checking on him. The vibration in his body climbed up his spine and settled in his skull. John told himself he was only anxious. Then he reasoned it away by being tired. The buzzing grew, and finally he pulled up to a rundown, roadside motel on the outskirts of Pensacola.

Checking in, he decided maybe a bite to eat would help. A ramshackle wood building sat on the other end of the lot. It looked like a bar, but it was early yet and there were several cars parked out front, so he hoped the place served food as well. He took his time trekking that way, to avoid tripping on the broken pieces of asphalt. By the time he pushed open the door, the buzzing had become a roar.

Every head turned to take him in and save one old man at the bar; they all watched him move slowly toward the bartender. John had already surmised the place had no food, but at this point he needed to sit down, so after an awkward climb onto a tall bar stool he ordered a beer.

"Got an ID on you?"

John shook his head. "Left it over at the hotel."

The man nodded. "That's too bad. I can't serve you without an ID."

"I'm old enough," John said.

"Maybe, but the law says I should card you."

"Give him a damn beer, Matt." It was the old man that spoke.

The bartender shook his head, but filled a mug from the tap. He sat the beer in front of the old man and said, "I'll put it on your tab, Jim. Reckon it's your business what you do with it."

The old man grabbed the freshly poured beer as well as his own highball glass and moved closer. He sat the beer in front of John before taking a seat that left only one spot between them. John tried to hand him a five, but the man waved it off. His hat read "Vietnam Vet."

"Thanks," John said and took a long drink of beer.

The man shook his head. "No, thank you."

When John stuffed the five in his right pocket his hand touched the coin Captain Rick had given him. Three beers in, the thrum inside his head faded away.

John slept well that night and the next morning got up and drove all the way to Waco. The cemetery was locked up for the night, so he found a hotel with a bar and checked in. For the second night he drank himself quiet.

He stayed there one week. Then two.

Part of every day, he spent at the cemetery staring down at the headstone of his brother. Over and over, he used his finger to trace the etching Spc. Austin Bayless, while trying to find his voice to explain. His tears fell fat and wet, and still John could not speak actual words. There were flowers in the vase and a little American flag, but no one came to the grave in all the hours John sat there. The buzz inside his brain became a constant each day, until he got back to the hotel and drank it away.

He drove by the house every evening. Idling down their street, at a speed reminiscent of the one he and Bayless covered so many miles together, John missed his fallen brother fiercely.

Sometimes a light or two was on in the house. Sometimes not.

That second Wednesday he saw them. They pulled into the driveway just as he came around the block. She paused and stared as he rolled by ever-so-slow. He could've kept going, but Bayless would've been angry if he had, and John had already done plenty to piss off his brother. So he squeezed the Jeep's hand brake and shifted into reverse.

The little family stood on the lawn and watched as he took his time swinging his legs out. Sitting on the ground at the cemetery left him stiff at the end of the day, so he moved extra slow.

"You're Hemingway," she said when he finally made it near enough.

Unwilling to trust his voice, he nodded. The oldest, the boy, chewed his lip and looked so much like his dad Hemingway had a hard time looking down at him. The girl clung to her momma's leg, but she too had Bayless's red hair.

He hoped they would remember their dad, but they

were young still, and Bayless had been gone damn near three years already. Before that he'd been deployed so how could they remember?

"Will you come in?"

Hemingway shook his head and took a deep breath. "I can't stay, but I wanted you to know your husband—he was my best friend."

She nodded.

"I'd bring him back if I could. He loved all of you." John fought the tears pressing into his one remaining eye.

She gulped air and sobbed. The kids only looked on.

"I know they gave your daddy one of these, but I want y'all to have mine too." Hemingway extended his arm and opened the fist clutching his Purple Heart. "That way you can each have one to remember your dad."

He lowered his hand and the youngest child took it.

"He earned them both. Then some."

That night he didn't sleep. The next morning John drove down to Fort Hood where he refilled his scripts. The Percocet did nothing for the buzzing headaches, but they helped with his hips and back.

He'd been thinking about driving out to San Diego to say his goodbyes to Sanchez, but he didn't even know for sure the Sergeant was buried there. Besides, he'd yet to find the words to say goodbye to Bayless.

He drove back to the cemetery where his friend was buried, but John didn't even get out of the Jeep. Again and again the words repeated in his mind. *I'm sorry.* But he lacked the courage to actually get out and say them. What good would it do anyway? Bayless was gone. And

John couldn't fix that. Not even if he was whole, instead of fucking guilt-ridden cripple.

He sat there a few hours rubbing that coin Captain Rick had given him, and staring out across the graveyard waiting for his gut to again speak.

His head buzzed, but his gut stayed silent, so John drove down by the river. The Brazos. Bayless had talked about the river as if it were the Nile, but it held no magic for John. No allure. Just dark water rolling slowly toward the Gulf of Mexico. He drove along the bank until he came to another cemetery. Much older than the one where they'd laid Bayless to rest.

His gut told him to park the Jeep.

A light drizzle fell as he strolled through the old graveyard. There were no fresh graves here. No American flags or plastic flowers. The grass was tall and unkempt and many of the stones were illegible. He paused to read the ones he could make out.

Emma Harrison Carter 1852-1874

Dead at twenty-two. John would turn twenty-two in a few weeks, and thanks to modern medicine he was still alive. By all rights, he should've died there beside his brothers.

No, he should have died instead of his brothers.

Alexander Clingman 1830-1870 "Loving Father"

Forty years old. Old Alex spent twice as long on earth as John had. Still a short life, especially by today's standards. John couldn't imagine what it would feel like to be forty. Or a father. Emily used to talk about having kids. Hell, she probably had one by now. John would never have any.

G. W. Johnson 1829-1865

The buzzing in John's head swelled to a roar. He stared down at the marker. He could almost feel the deaths of those buried here. Emma in childbirth. Clingman to disease. G.W. Johnson? He took his own life.

John was losing it. Imagining shit he had no way of knowing. The fucking buzzing in his skull had turned into a full out roar. He had to get away from here. From this cemetery. From this town. He'd spent too damn much time hanging out with dead people all day. Trying to wish them alive. And why? Nothing about this life was right or fair, especially not the fact that he was still walking around in it, albeit on metal spindles that left him aching at the end of each day. He'd drink himself to sleep and wake stiff in the morning only to do it all again the same godforsaken way tomorrow. Maybe the grave was better.

Ware and Jennings were up in Missouri. Back at Fort Leonard Wood after a second deployment. John talked to them now and again, but they had a new band of brothers now and last thing they needed was a reminder of what could go wrong.

John strapped his reminders on every single morning. Not that he needed them for that. The realization of what he'd let happen never left his mind.

He reached back in his pocket and clutched the relic Captain Rick had given him, as he stared down at G.W. Johnson's tombstone, wondering what the "G.W." stood for. Not that it mattered. The man had been in the ground better than a century. A speck of time compared to the years the coin had seen. He wasn't sure whether to believe the story about it coming from Hemingway or not, but either way the coin had outlived most of the hands to touch it. How many more lives would come and go before this small chunk of hammered metal ceased to exist?

Another worthless pondering, though it led John to wonder what would become of his legs once the rest of him was gone. They would outlast him, that much was for sure. Just like the coral shells that made up the Florida Keys had outlasted their living body. John had put it off a long time, but now his gut told him there was only one place left to visit.

Paradise.

He made it all the way to New Orleans the first day, before the buzz wore him down. A bottle of rum and a bourbon street whore convinced him to stay a second night. He awoke alone in a cheap hotel room the next morning, but still was in no hurry to leave the city and head for Key West, so he drove down to the French Quarter, where he sat and ate beignets and drank chicory. The church bells across the way shook through the fog of his hangover with more clarity than the coffee brought him.

Crossing the street he made his way across Jackson Square under a low, gray sky. A fortune teller called to

him, but the slippery, uneven bricks forced him to focus on the ground, so Hemingway ignored her offer of
prophecy.

Inside the church, he put money in a box and lit two
candles.

One for Sanchez.

One for Bayless.

Not that he believed they would do any good, but
for the souls of his fallen brothers, John would try anything.

He studied the rosaries in the gift shop. None were
made of coral like the one Emily had given him, but one
claimed to contain water drawn from a spring in Lourdes
where The Virgin Mary was said to have appeared. John
bought that one and accepted a blessing from the priest
who rung him up. He hung it around his neck, even as
the priest frowned at him.

It felt good, reassuring somehow to again have a rosary around his neck. In another life he could've stayed
in a place like New Orleans forever, but in this one, John
could stave off paradise only so long. Outside the fortune teller again called to him.

He kept walking.

He made it to the other side of Jackson before he
saw them—a young couple getting married in the court-
yard. A simple, little ceremony. Just the young man, the
girl, and a gaunt minister with long, yellow curls of hair.
They were young. Couldn't have been even twenty years
old, John guessed.

What caught his eye was how the two stood in such
striking contrast to one another. The young girl delicate

and lovely. Angelic, John thought. Her blond hair partially pulled up and pinned in the back, the rest falling down and resting gently on petite shoulders. Her skin, what little was uncovered, was light pink and powdery, like rose petals. The dress was simple but pretty, and it shined bright white. From the looks of her innocence, John assumed she deserved to wear the white.

The young man, on the other hand, had a vividly different look about him. His hair could not have been more black. It hung fine and straight in a way to frame his face. His skin was brown, but John couldn't really tell his ethnicity. And even with one eye, from a distance, John could see his piercing, gray eyes, looking up at the minister.

With an increased gusto the man practically shouted, "In as much as Billy and Jenny have consented together in wedlock and have witnessed the same before this company, and pledged their vows to each other, by the authority vested in me by the State of Louisiana, I now pronounce you husband and wife." With a knowing smile and a dramatic bow, the minister said, "Billy, you may kiss your bride."

John clapped when they did just that, and the sweet, young girl looked up and blushed bright red.

John started to walk away but stopped. Something in his gut turned him back toward the couple. The young man looked up, his steely gray eyes met John's gaze. John pulled the coin from his pocket and tossed it to the boy. The kid caught it and studied its features just as John had done. A puzzling, almost incredulous look washed over the groom. "This coin," he said. "Where did you get it?"

"An old friend gave it to me. He said it would bring luck. Hope it favors you more than it has me," John said before he walked away.

Behind him the boy kept talking, but John hobbled on.

He heard the bride ask, "Billy, what is it?"

"I just think I've seen this before," came a quiet reply. John heard nothing more, as he left the newlyweds behind.

Leaving the city, he headed east along the coast, but he was tired and worn out from his weeks on the road. Eating too much shitty food. Drinking too much. Thinking too much.

Something was alive inside his head, buzzing around, but damned if he could describe it. Or quiet it. Only booze helped, so come late afternoon he stopped at the same bar in Pensacola. The Vietnam vet was nowhere to be found, but the bartender seemed to remember him, so he didn't hassle John this time.

John almost wished he had. In a foul mood, he would've told him he left it overseas, along with his legs and his goddamned eye. Instead, he sat in silence and drank several beers. With his headache only dulled, John returned to his room where he slept in fits and starts. Restlessness drove him out of bed early, and he was back on the road before the sun.

He drove hard and steady, but still late afternoon was on him before he hit Manatee Bay at the edge of the mainland.

Highway 1.

The Keys.

His body buzzed and his skull hummed, but at long last he'd returned to paradise.

Twilight fell before he made it down to Key West. He pulled up at the apartments he once called home with exhaustion riding shotgun. Still, John was determined to make a stand. Even on two glorified carbon fiber stilts.

Stairs were hell, and the place had no elevator, so he sat on his ass and bumped his way up to the second floor. Sweating and shaking when he reached the top, he'd come home at last.

Not for long though. He knocked once, then walked inside as if he'd been there only yesterday.

His dad and Lito stood from the table. "John," his father said.

"John died. A long time ago." He walked by them, headed for his old room. He was counting on it still being in there.

It wasn't.

Neither was his bed. Damn it. He needed that bottle. Not only to quiet the buzz in his head, but to make a symbolic statement to his dad.

But a fucking computer, a desk, and ratty old roll-around chair took up most of the room. They'd moved on as if he never fucking existed in this space. Just as well.

"John what are you doing? Where have you been? Everybody is worried about you. We've been looking for you."

"Who? Mom. She doesn't give a shit. Probably needs more pain pills."

"No son, I've been looking for you."

Hemingway laughed. "Yeah, I see that. You found me. And from your kitchen chair. Guess you're right again. Go ahead lay another I told you so on me."

His father's mouth moved, but no words came out.

"Where's my stuff?"

The elder Rivero pointed to a handful of boxes against the far wall.

Hemingway found what he'd come for in the second box.

His dad was still standing there in the doorway, when he squeezed by with the bottle of bourbon dangling in his hand. "I knew you wouldn't toss out a gift from Captain Rick. Aye Aye Captain." He saluted once, and left the apartment without another word.

The victory proved short lived.

There is no dignified way to bump down two flights of stairs, while holding a bottle of whiskey, but that's exactly what John had to do. He heard the door open behind him so he knew his dad, or Lito, or both, were up there watching.

Waiting.

From the top step, his father called out. "Where are you going?"

Hemingway did not answer, and he did not look back. He was done answering to his father. Done answering to anyone. At least on this earth. He'd never been religious like Emily, but still he hoped there was something more than this world offered. Though looking for it had cost him everything.

"Don't leave like this. There are people here who care about you. People who want to see you."

Still John said nothing. Not even when his dad said, "At least go see Emily. Please. She lives in her parents' old place"

Gritting his teeth, John waited until his heart calmed before pulling himself to his feet at the bottom of the steps. He refused to let his dad know the impact of hearing Emily's name aloud was indeed a painful blow.

Shut up, Boy. Take their best shot without letting 'em know they hurt you. Captain Rick's voice echoed in his ears, and the long ago gifted whiskey called to him, but John wouldn't slake his thirst. Not yet. Not before he faced his last tormentor.

The house was lit up. It was one of the old style places with a big porch. He knocked hoping she would be the one to answer, but of course he didn't get that lucky.

A man walked to the door. It wasn't Caleb Pendleton. John was half relieved, half angry there would be no exchange between them. Instead Mike Herrera opened the screen door and took a step forward. Mike was an acquaintance, not quite a friend. He had poured countless cups of coffee for John and their friends, back in high school.

"Hello John," Mike said warmly. "Emily will be really glad to see you. Come on in, let me get her."

He disappeared around the corner and John found himself bathed in a cloud of emotion and confusion. A couple minutes later, Emily rounded the door, her eyes already filled with tears. Mike stood behind her, holding a baby boy.

"John." Emily wrapped her arms around him.

John stood motionless as her tears dampened his shirt.

Finally she pulled back and sized him up from the eyepatch around his head, to the pant legs that wrinkled in such a way as to show there were no legs to fill them out. Though she looked older, Emily was as pretty as ever. He stood before her, a wreck of a man. Scared and incomplete, he felt much like the unsure boy she'd handed those rosary beads to so long ago.

John looked across the room at the sleeping baby Mike held. "You and Caleb's kid?"

"John, Caleb was a mistake," she softly replied. "After you, I made a lot of them."

Emily motioned to Mike, and he handed her the baby boy.

"I told you you'd be better off without me. What's his name?" John nodded at the child.

"Ryland," she said. "But we call him Rye."

John nodded. "Good solid name. Makes me think of whiskey." He reached inside his collar and pulled out the rosary he'd bought for himself in New Orleans. He gently draped it over Emily's head. The beads pooled on the baby's stomach. "I lost the ones you gave me. I got these blessed by a priest in New Orleans."

Hemingway turned and walked back out the front door to the porch. Behind him Emily began to cry again, and he couldn't take that so he hobbled down the three steps grateful they weren't so steep or long that he would have to again bump down them on his ass. He kept moving even when she called his name. "John!"

"Ryland John," She said. "His middle name is John."

He reached the Jeep as the buzz inside his skull screeched and screamed. He saw Emily stop at the edge of her yard, watching him, but still he twisted the cap and took a long hard pull from the bottle. Emily glanced back, and Mike walked up behind her. John took one more pull from the bottle and then waved once before pulling away.

The weeks out on the road had left him tired, worn out, and nearly broke. He needed sleep and he needed it now, but rooms were too damn high in this town so he drove up to Big Pine Key. To a crappy little roadside motel he once took Emily to. The night they were supposed to be at prom.

It seemed like a good idea, given it was cheap and far enough away no one was likely to know him. But when he checked in and lay back on the bed, a flood of memories poured in. He drained half the bourbon and still that fucking buzz raged on inside his skull. Sanchez, Bayless, his father, Captain Rick, the broken mess that was his mother, the pretty little life Emily had made for herself after he'd made her let him go, and the new one she'd brought into this world. He felt no place for himself.

He hadn't eaten much all day, so he was more than a little drunk when he slid open the drawer and pulled out the bible. He tried to read for a while, but none of the words made it through the thunderheads inside his mind. Reading had been hard since the explosion. A few pages and his eye would tire, making it hell to focus on the empty promises printed on the pages in front of him.

In a clap of rage, he flung the book against the far

wall. The bible landed with the pages all askew.

The Gideons.

He added them to the list of everyone else he'd let down.

He took the legs off next. One after the other he tossed them toward the bible.

The contents of the bourbon disappeared drink by drink down his throat and still it all swirled inside the eddy of his brain. The humming, the disappointment, the fear, the anger, the regret, the shame. That was the source of the noise. The pieces of him scraping against each other in the vortex of his failures.

Only one thing would quiet the storm.

That's where paradise lay. In the quiet dark of nothing.

Paradise could not be built upon the dead and the dying. Mother Nature had tried. Uncle Sam had tried, but utopia could not, would not grow from death.

Another day in paradise? John could not. Would not.

He pulled that bottle of Percocet from his camouflage coat. Softly singing the words to "Paradise By the Dashboard Light," he swallowed the pills one after another.

Trouble in paradise? That came when both the bourbon and the pills were gone.

The fear stayed with him right until the end, when he lay back on that bed in that cheap roadside motel and closed his eyes.

Only then, did the buzzing stop.

Hemingway
by Dan Johnson

John was a soldier, from deep down in Florida,
He turned eighteen on Key West.
The Army would get him, and as soon as they let him,
He signed on the line to enlist.

They all called him Hemingway, because he spent every day,
Cussing and fighting and drunk.
And lord, he could tell you a story so well,
You'd get wrapped in the yarns that he spun.

So Hemingway tell us a tale,
Of some great adventure, of champions or fishermen,
Or girls that put wind in men's sails.
Take us away. Hey Hemingway.

On the day that he turned nineteen, that cursed IED,
Took off his legs at the thigh.
Mangled and burned up but thankful it turned out,
The doctors at least saved one eye.

Then they sent him home to his mom on the coast,
They said "Thanks for your service there, son.
This Purple Heart is a medal to mark all the good
for your country you've done."

Through his personal hell, not a soul would he tell,
To modest to speak of his pain.
While innocent, ignorant, well-meaning friends of his,
Said it would all be okay.

So he just kept on swinging, as each blow kept sting-
ing,
Not sure how much longer he'd fight.
And everyone asked him to tell us what happened,
That day he almost lost his life.

So Hemingway tell us a tale,
Of some great adventure, the battles the missions,
The glory and how you prevailed.
What do you say? Hey Hemingway.

Last Saturday night, as the vacancy sign,
Beckoned to him from the road.
With a bottle of bourbon and a month's worth of
Percocet,
Tucked in his camouflage coat.

He reached for the Bible, and he read for a while.
But nothing much seemed to stand out.
So in that little hotel room, when the Gideons fell
through,
He took the Hemingway out.

So Hemingway tell us a tale,
Of the young life they took from you,
The darkness you're going through,
How we and the whole world have failed.
There as you lay, oh Hemingway.
There as you lay, oh Hemingway.

Heirloom

Inspired by the song "Bloom" by Dan Johnson

She stood in the backyard, amid the cloying scent of roses, and watched his plane rise into a cloudless blue sky. Her heart fluttered like the butterflies that flocked here to her mother's garden. She brought her right hand, the one clutching her phone, up against the spot where she imagined her damaged heart to be.

Like most aspects of her imagination, Emily Atwell's aim was slightly off, so that her hand rested solidly against her left breast. Her heart, like every other human's, at least of average design, lay more in the center of her chest. But Emily did not want to think of herself as average. And she absolutely did not want to live an average life.

Anyone else would realize that Emily most certainly did not live an average life. She stood in paradise, beneath an azure sky, in the backyard of a million dollar home, surrounded by one of the world's most extensive collections of exotic, and rare rose vines, shrubs, and ornamental trees. But Emily did not care about her mother's lifelong hobby, her dad's wealth, or the fact she was fortunate enough to call Key West home.

Emily cared only about a boy.

A boy that had just fled paradise on a plane bound for Missouri and her only link to him was the phone she clutched in her clammy palm.

His last text message sent her heart into desperate flutters of anxiety because he was leaving, yet it also lifted her spirits. She found hope in the beauty of his words. *Thx for the send off and the blessing. Love the pic. Pls send one of your smile too. Every soldier needs a pretty girl to stare at when he gets homesick.*

He loved her. He really loved her. No, he hadn't spelled it out word for word, but she knew John well and he did not part with emotion easily.

That was okay because Emily knew they were soul mates. They'd dated since April of their junior year. Fourteen months in all. Fourteen months that felt like both a blink in time, and forever, all at once.

Now he was going to be gone even longer. Ten weeks for basic training. Then five months for some other kind of training. Then he would be shipped over there. To look for roadside bombs. She couldn't let her mind dwell on that. Not with her chest about to explode as she stood here under a vast empty sky. His plane didn't even have the decency to leave a trail behind, so just like that he was gone.

She should've gone to the airport to see him off. But he hadn't wanted that. They should've gotten married before he left. He hadn't wanted that either.

Emily exhaled and brought her focus down from the heavens to the backyard. What about the things she wanted? Why hadn't he cared about her needs and wants?

She for damned sure didn't want him to enlist. He didn't need to. He could've kept working for Captain Rick, just like his father. Or even better, he could have gone to work for her father. They could've lived here on this island forever, but now that he was gone, she too yearned to escape. Her parents had wanted her to enroll at the University of Georgia, like they had. But Emily persuaded them she needed a year off from school.

They hadn't liked the idea, but she'd insisted, because she assumed John would be here too. And if he was staying in Key West, so was she.

But he hadn't stayed, and now she was stuck here. Alone.

She stood there tasting salty tears, until she caught her breath and the ache inside her beat less frantic. Even after her heart slowed and her eyes dried, Emily's stomach felt as empty as the sky above.

Now what?

Her dad was off at the golf club, playing or drinking or flirting with that redheaded waitress. Her mom was in her greenhouse, grafting various roots together in her ever-continuing quest to create the perfect rose. They knew John was leaving this morning. They knew she'd spent most of last night, and the better part of the last week crying, but they offered no real sympathy. Instead, they were glad to see him go.

Her parents weren't racists in the overt, "You can

only date a white, Anglo, rich-boy kind of way." No, her mother especially was too mired in the Catholic Church for such an outlook. But they were the, "I don't think that boy is right for you." kind of racists that said subtle things like, "The military is a good place for a boy like him," and "Be happy for John. He will get to experience things and see places his family could never provide."

Her dad liked John well enough when he was the star running back, but he didn't much like the idea of his daughter being tied to a dark, Cuban fisherman. And now that his football days were over, that was all John had waiting for him here in Key West.

John loved the water, but Emily did not. Oh, she liked to look at it, and listen to the waves roll in. Sometimes she even waded in just enough to let it lap at her ankles, but she didn't like the way the tide sucked the sand out from under her feet when she got too far out, and she certainly did not enjoy getting up early and sitting quietly while looking for fish moving along the surface.

John had taken her and tried to teach her, but no part of it felt like fun to her. And she resented how much time he spent out there, even when he wasn't working. Just for his own pleasure.

He'd joined the Army for the same selfish reasons. Because he wanted to go off and do something, he said.

Something alone.

Without her.

He hadn't added that last part, but Emily knew what he meant. He'd broken up with her once, right after they'd had that scare. Turned out she'd only been late, but John completely freaked those four or five days. They got back together after a week or so, but things hadn't really been the same for them since.

Now Emily wished she had been pregnant. They would have gotten married, and John would've stayed, and her belly would be nice and round by now.

She'd gone to her priest to confess her sin, and he'd instructed her to pray the rosary as well as the novena to St. Therese. Somebody heard her prayers, God granted exactly what she asked for, but Emily knew that we all pray for the wrong things at times. The pain in her chest for John told her she'd chose the wrong prayers.

But John would come back to her. He must. She simply could not picture life without him. To make certain, she vowed to write him letters every single day, to call once the Army let him have that privilege. And she would send him the picture he'd asked for–right after she washed the tear streaks from her face and did her hair and make-up. A soldier like John needed a perfect picture to stare at when he missed home.

And so she did. She wrote letters every single day that first week, but she didn't mail any of them. The first few days she was sad and lonely, because he hadn't even called when he landed. He'd told her he couldn't use the phone those first few weeks, but he could've called from the airport at the very least. He could have, if he'd truly wanted. The sad turned to mad, but the lonely ache persisted on, and that pissed her off all the more. She kept writing letters, but her pride wouldn't let her send them, not until he contacted her first.

Let him wonder what she was doing. Let him question her commitment. Let John assume she'd moved on without a single thought.

Nineteen days after Emily watched John's plane disappear into the sky, her mom flung open the curtains beside the bed to expose yet another brilliant, blue morning. Emily squinted against the harsh light.

"You, Little Missy, need to get up and get moving. It's time you stopped living like a vampire in this cave."

"Why?"

"Because we're going shopping for a whole new wardrobe for the trip."

Emily pulled a pillow up over her dark curls. "What trip?"

"Rome. I finally convinced your father to take me to see the Vatican."

"Seriously?" Emily sat up in bed. "Dad is taking you to Italy?"

"Not me. Us. Now hurry scurry and get ready. I have big plans for us."

Italy would be kind of cool, and a new wardrobe sounded good, but still, Emily felt so lethargic. Even in the shower she struggled to muster much enthusiasm.

Until she came downstairs and found the letter,

> *Hey Em,*
>
> *Sorry I haven't written. Been cra zy here. Not a lot to report.*
>
> *They're working our asses off and it's so damn hot. Different than there. No cool breeze. Just hot heavy air that makes the dirt and grass and grit cling to your skin.*

I miss your skin. I stare at the pictures you sent when I can but we aren't supposed to use our phones. I graduate Basic in a couple weeks. Wish you could be here for it, but I know that's impossible. Once my AI training starts I should get a few more freedoms.

Will write or call soon.

John

Still no *Love, John* or even an *I miss you, John* to sign off, but he had written *I miss your skin.* She was made up of skin, so in John's reluctant way that was the same as saying I miss you.

And he wished she could be at his graduation. Why couldn't she be? She should be there. She needed to be there. Damn it. She would be there. For him. No one else would go. If she didn't go John would probably be the only soldier there with no family to hug his neck and tell him how proud they were. Her parents would never let her fly all the way to Missouri by herself to see John. They didn't even like John. All of it swirled in her mind. She tried to concentrate while shopping, but in her mind, Missouri now seemed more exotic than Italy.

Part of her was still angry, so the idea of showing up unexpectedly appealed to her. She could tell him off in spectacular fashion and then relent to letting him wrap those strong arms around her. God she missed those strong arms. And other parts of him too. They'd had sex a few times the weeks before he left, but he'd pulled away those last days. Barely said a word, even when she tried to entice him. Surely, after weeks of hard work, surrounded by nothing but other guys, he'd be more inclined. Maybe they could even get married while she was there. What was more romantic than that? She would still miss him, but missing him as Mrs. John Rivero didn't seem as pathetic as missing him as his high school girlfriend.

After doing research on the internet, she worked up a plan in her mind. She couldn't buy a plane ticket on her credit card, because her daddy got alerts anytime she spent more than seventy-five dollars. Eventually she would have to take out more cash than that, but by then it would be too late for him to stop her.

On the big day, she lifted the spare key off the hook by the garage door, and tossed her two bags in the trunk of her Dad's Lexus. Her parents were still asleep, and she was afraid the garage door would wake them, so to bolster her odds, she left it open after she backed out. With an hour until sunup, she headed north up Interstate 1. She didn't really breathe easy until she hit the mainland. She spotted two cop cars along the way and worried that maybe her dad had already discovered his car gone and alerted the authorities, but no one stopped her. Easy as that, she was in Miami. Emily figured she was safe then, with so many cars and routes to take. She set the cruise for exactly the speed limit and drove on anxious to erase the miles between her and John.

About eight-thirty her phone started ringing. First her mom. Then her dad. She ignored both. She'd left a note that said all she intended to say.

I'm leaving town for a few days, but I will be back. Don't worry, I'm fine. Sorry about the car, Dad, but I knew you'd say no and I have to do this.

She stopped a few times to stretch her legs, and once to get gas. A little after noon, she got hungry and stopped in at a Chili's in Kissimmee. She'd never before sat in a restaurant by herself and eaten alone. Doing so left her feeling anxious and antsy and nervous about the trip for the first time. In the restroom, she noticed a new zit above her right temple so instead of a coke and the sweet raspberry vinaigrette salad she craved, Emily opted for water and a minuscule bit of ranch.

She silently prayed to Saint Drogo to make the pimple go away and to Saint Dwynwen as the patron to lovers. Saint Valentine had already let her down too many times, so she left him out of her prayers.

Emily had hoped to make it to Atlanta that first day, or at least somewhere close so she would be near halfway to Missouri, but by the time she crossed over into Georgia, it was late afternoon and she was bored out of her skull. In an apparent act of punishment, her dad had disabled the satellite radio. She'd scrolled through the FM stations a dozen times without finding any good music.

She hadn't told any of her friends she was leaving, much less where she was going, but Emily was getting equally sleepy and fidgety. She knew she would go completely mental, if she didn't talk to someone, so she dialed her friend Bethany. The sun was brutal in her eyes, even with the visor pulled down. Bethany didn't answer, and her voicemail was full. So after Emily ended the call, she texted ... *Hey girl call me asap*

When the airbag exploded it knocked her phone from her hand and chipped her tooth. The blow also broke her nose, blackened both eyes, and left an angry bruise on her left shoulder to go along with a wickedly intense concussion.

"All in all she's very lucky," so said the state trooper to her parents that next day. The day she was supposed to arrive in Missouri. Instead, she was at a hospital in Valdosta, Georgia. The trooper wrote her out a ticket, there in the hospital room—a whole day after. Like she hadn't suffered enough.

Emily didn't really remember much about the accident, but apparently traffic had been stopped, and between the sun in her eyes and the phone in her hand she'd failed to notice, before plowing into the back end of a fifth-wheel camper. Luckily no one else was hurt, but both her dad's Lexus, and the camping trailer were totaled.

They flew back to Key West. Even though she could tell her dad was pissed, he didn't completely lose his shit until they were ensconced back in their Victorian bungalow, nestled amongst all of her mother's fancy roses.

He sat on the edge of the bed and put one hand on her ankle. His grip firm, but not tight, he said, "No more, Emily. That boy is—is gone. Let him go. Even if he comes back, he's not right for you. Your mother and I love you, and we're not going to sit back and watch you throw your life away on some punk kid just because he could run the football in high school."

"John is—"

"Gone is what he is." He squeezed her ankle harder. "I'm telling you right now. It's over between you and him. When I get you a new phone, I'm going to block his number, and I'll also be checking to see who you're calling and texting. Forget that boy, or else."

"Or else what?" She wanted to be angry and defiant, but tilting her chin back hurt too much, so she sounded more like a bratty toddler than the independent woman she yearned to be.

"Don't push me on this, Emily." Roger Atwell flexed his jaws. "Don't force my hand." Her dad removed his hand and stared out the window for a few minutes before saying. "My company owns the building his father lives in. I've got leverage in places you don't even understand. Or I could always call in debts from Captain Rick. I can and will ruin that family if it comes to that." He stood and walked to the doorway before adding. "Don't make me tear apart a family to save you from yourself. For once Emily, don't be selfish, just because you think you know what you want. Trust me. You won't want a boy like that in another few years." It was painful to cry, but Emily couldn't hold back the sobs.

Half an hour or so after he left, her mother came in. She doted and fussed and even put a vase of fresh cut pink roses on bedside the table. Emily of course recognized the petals as her namesake variety. They were her mom's favorite.

Being named after her mom's favorite Rose was a

mixed bag. They really were lovely, and she knew how much her mother adored them, but sometimes Emily felt like just another pretty addition to her mom's collection. As if she could be trained and pruned to bloom, in just the way her mom wanted.

Her mom loved to tell her the story of how they hadn't known whether she was going to be a boy or girl until the day she was born. They didn't have names picked out, but her mom secretly hoped she was a girl and wanted to name her Rose. When the nurse laid her newborn baby in her arms, she looked down and thought her infant daughter was more beautiful than any rose she'd ever seen, so she gave her the name "Emily" to remind her she was her mother's favorite thing.

"Did dad come speak to you?"

Emily rolled her eyes as an answer. And now it would be her mom's turn to reinforce her dad's sentiments. To remind her of her roots and make certain she understood she was grafted to their little version of perfection.

Terri Atwell sighed deeply and began her cultivation. "I know you're not supposed to say things like this to someone who's upset, but I know how you feel honey."

Emily shook her head. "Just stop, Mom. I already know what you're going to say and trust me, you have no idea how I feel."

Her mom smiled. "I know a lot more than you assume. You and I are not all that different, no matter what you think."

A full minute ticked by, before her mom spoke

again. "I didn't always love your father. I'm so thankful God brought us together, because he's given me a life better than I ever imagined. And he's given me you. But when I was your age, I wanted someone else."

Emily sat up in the bed. "Who?"

Again her mom took a while before she answered. "His name was Will. Will Harrison. I was so enamored with him. Back then I would've staked my life he was my one true love."

"I thought," Emily paused and shook her head. "You and Dad. I thought you were like these amazing college sweethearts."

Her mother chuckled. "That's the way your dad tells the story, and I'm glad he does. Really I was a naïve little girl pretending I knew what I was doing. We only talk about the sweet parts because that's all either of us wants to dwell on."

"So what really happened?"

When her mom stood, Emily feared her mom was going to leave without telling her, but instead she went to the doorway and peeked outside into the hall before pulling the door shut. After sitting back on the edge of the bed she said, "I've always told you fairytale love is a real thing, because I want you to go out and find it, but the truth is love is never easy or straightforward or without complication. True love is real, but you won't be able to recognize it until you're completely comfortable with yourself and your own wants and dreams. Don't tie them to another person, because eventually that person will disappoint you. Especially if you're already disappointed in yourself."

"Okay fine. I get that mom. But what about you and this Will guy?"

"I met him my first day on campus, at freshman orientation. He was so good-looking. Had this thick wavy hair that hung down to his shoulders. He looked just like Matthew McConaughey."

Emily giggled but caught herself.

"Will was so full of life. His laugh filled the entire room. I melted the instant I saw him." Her mom shook her head. "I met your father the same day. Or night actually. There was a big party. Your father tried so hard. Too hard probably. And he was just too smooth. Too clean and pressed. Then there was Will over in the corner with his guitar. His worn-out jeans fit him like a glove. He had three days worth of scruff, and he didn't even say one word to me. Just kept playing that guitar and staring back at me. I'd never seen a man with so much intent in his eyes."

Emily had never seen her mother look so girlish. "So what did you do?"

"Your father went to get me another drink. Trash can punch in solo cups." She rolled her eyes and wrinkled her nose. "Everybody there was getting drunk, and I was right there with them. So I walked over to that corner where Will was playing, and I let my one finger," She held up her right index finger. "I let it trail just ever so slightly along his jawline as I walked by."

"Mom!" Emily scooted closer.

Blushing, her mom said, "I'm telling you he was that gorgeous."

Emily tried to picture the scene, but conjuring up

thoughts of her mom drunk on trashcan punch hitting on some hot musician seemed as out of place as a dandelion amid her sea of roses. "Did you guys..." she trailed off, too embarrassed by the possibilities to finish her question.

But her mom took a deep breath and answered anyway. "He met me outside. Didn't say a word. Just kissed me. It seemed like forever. When I finally looked up, your dad was standing there in the porch light with two cups in his hand. I could see his heart breaking, but I didn't care. I didn't owe him anything. And I'd never felt as alive as I did in that moment."

Taking Emily's hand, her mom held it tightly. Emily was surprised by how warm her mother's palm was up against her own.

"So what happened?"

"We fell in love. But I hid it him from your grandparents. They never would've accepted somebody like Will. He was a wild, free spirit. His mom was a hairdresser, and his dad wasn't around at all.

Will was brilliant in a way I can't really explain. He wasn't much of a student really, but it was sort of clear he could do whatever he wanted, even if it wasn't the smart or maybe the right thing to do. I just felt so caught up when we were together.

I think it really hurt him that I wouldn't take him back to Buckhead with me on the weekends, when I went home. But other than that, the whole year was perfect. Will started to really make a name for himself writing songs and playing all over Georgia and South Carolina on weekends. Even Tennessee sometimes, and Florida during spring break."

Emily was torn between her fascination over this side of her mother she'd never known, and her agitation over the fact that there had to be some big life lesson coming. "So what happened? Did he break your heart and leave you for the road or something?"

"It did end badly." Her mom let go of her hand before continuing. "But not like you think. We ended up in a lot of trouble. There was a new mall opening up in Atlanta, and they were building this big beautiful hotel right next to it. They were putting a waterfall with live trees and foliage in the atrium. So one night Will and I drove over. We broke into the place to see it. After we got inside we dropped some acid and—"

"You did what?"

"I told you, I was a lot wilder then, Emily."

She couldn't remember her mother ever being so candid. "Yeah, but wild for you would be like backseat sex or something. Now you're like breaking in and taking acid! I just didn't think...I mean oh my God, mom!"

"Don't take the Lord's name in vain, Emily. We were in the atrium, pretending like we were in a jungle. I think we thought we were Adam and Eve. When the police showed up we were both naked. Actually we were...you know, in the act."

"Gross mom." Emily shook off the mental image. "Spare me a few details."

"Anyway, they arrested us. Your grandparents nearly disowned me. Still, it was worse for Will. When they arrested us, Will had quite a bit of pot on him and he already had a prior conviction for selling. I was high and scared and naked and I all I really remember is Will telling the cops it was all his drugs, all his idea, all him. He ended up doing three years over in Macon."

"Did you ever see him again?"

"Your grandparents wouldn't let me even mention his name, but when school started again I wrote him a few letters. He only wrote back once. He wasn't nice, but what he said was true. That letter showed me all of his anger and hurt over us getting arrested and me never taking him back to Buckhead to meet my family or friends. Prison changed him, and I could tell in that one letter he wasn't the same."

Then she fell quiet and said, "But yes I did see him once. I felt guilty so I looked him up. He'd been out for a few years by then, and I was already married to your dad. He was playing at a club in Atlanta. A place I would never go, but I went anyway."

She rubbed her fingers across the Virgin Mary pendant around her neck a good long while before saying. "He was broken. I could tell, when I listened to him play. He wasn't that wild and free, beautiful boy I knew. I guess if you didn't know him before, you might think he was handsome in a way. I just remember watching him sing his songs and smoke cigarettes. He drank whiskey until he was slurring his words between the songs. But when he played, his fingers still moved so smooth and perfect. And when he sang, you could feel the pain in him. At the end, I worked up the courage to go talk to him. I walked up to the stage, and he just stared at me. I said, 'Hello Will,' and after a minute, he finished the whiskey in his glass and just said, 'What the fuck do you want?'"

"Oh Mom, that's awful," Emily said.

Her mom nodded. "I didn't even answer. I just left as fast as I could.

Then last year out of nowhere, my old roommate from freshman year sent me a link to his obituary. It hit me really hard, but I couldn't tell anyone. I guess, he basically drank himself to death."

Emily saw the sadness in her mother's eyes. "Mom, I'm so sorry."

"Me too, sweetheart. He made some bad choices that wrecked his life, and probably, I was one of them. At least in his eyes. After I got arrested, your grandparents kept a tight rein on me. I took your father home, because I knew they would approve. He came from a stable, well-heeled family. Old money my daddy liked to say. I was furious, but looking back it really was the best thing. I'm thankful I found your father, even if it took me years to truly appreciate him. Still, I'm not going to treat you like my parents treated me. But I am going to tell you I learned my lesson the hard way, and I would really love it if you learned from my mistakes instead of making your own. Sometimes people are just too different to make it work. It's not so much where you come from, but where you want to go. Will and I had different destinations, and I feel really certain that's the case with you and John as well."

Her mom was wrong, but Emily kept quiet. She appreciated her mother confiding in her, but John was not into drugs. He drank some, but who didn't. And John had gone into the Army, not prison. Emily said, "Thank you for telling me all of that, Mom," and left it at that.

Emily recovered from the wreck in a matter of weeks, but the loss of her father's trust lingered on. He kept a watchful eye, but still she continued to write John letters. She kept the letters hidden and mailed them secretly, whenever she could find an excuse to be away from the house.

John's letters back were nowhere near as frequent as hers. That was a mixed blessing since it reduced the chances of her dad intercepting one. Still, his infrequent contact seemed to reinforce her mother's speech about them having different destinations. Her mom did find a few of the letters and faithfully brought them, unopened, to Emily, always saying the same thing. "He finally wrote back."

How her mom even knew about all the letters she mailed, Emily didn't know. But her resolve stayed strong, and she clung to her belief that she would marry John and prove them all wrong.

With John gone, it didn't take long for other boys to start hitting her up. More than a few came around at her parents urging. Especially Caleb.

Emily wanted no part of Caleb, or any of the others. Her parents however, were on a mission. So she wasn't surprised to find him at her house when she returned from one of her clandestine forays to the post office. There he sat, perched on her veranda rail, chatting with her mom.

She shot her mom a look and hurried through the living room to the kitchen. Behind her, she heard her mom say, "Let me fix you a glass of sweet tea for stopping by."

Emily pounced the second her mom stepped into the kitchen. "What is he doing here?"

"Shhh." She held her finger to her lips. "He'll hear you," her mom whispered in her admonishing, Southern tone.

"Like I care."

Her mom arched a brow. "He interrupted his day to come here to see you. Meanwhile, you're busy chasing a boy that is too busy to so much as mail you a letter."

"I love John."

"Does he love you?"

"Okay fine, he doesn't write me back. But he also doesn't wear pink polos and white shorts. My God mom, Caleb is so cliché it's ridiculous!"

Her mother clicked her tongue, "I think he's handsome!"

"Mom, he's not even very smart," Emily retorted.

"Well he's polite, and he's a good Catholic boy. And he might not be the brightest bulb in the bathroom, but he sure looks good in the mirror. I don't care what color his shorts are. I just know he fills them out pretty well." Her mom raised her eyebrows and winked at Emily.

"Oh, my, God. You didn't just say that, Mom."

"Don't take the Lord's name in vain, Emily. Anyhow, I've invited him to have dinner tomorrow night at the club with us. It will go a long way to making your father happy, if he thinks you're trying to broaden your horizons."

Emily fumed, but her mother would not let this go. Nor would she uninvite Caleb. If Emily refused to go eat at the club, they would make her life hell by taking away what little freedom she had left. "Fine. I'll go tomorrow, but I'm not entertaining him today." She trudged out to the backyard with as much indignation as she could, given she'd just relented control of her life.

The dinner went off largely without a hitch. Emily had made up her mind to be on her best behavior in order to avoid ridicule from her mother and father. Her plan had been to be so overtly sugary sweet, Caleb would find her phony and superficial. But the thicker she laid it on, the more enamored he seemed to be. Finally, when he recounted his latest Regatta triumph, she crumbled and said, "Little boys and their boats."

At the disdain in her voice, her father made that sucking sound with his teeth and folded his arms across his chest. Her mother cocked her head like a parrot, and her eyes widened with intensity. Emily caved and said, "Caleb how about you and I go for a stroll down by the beach."

Her mother smiled and Caleb quickly agreed. Her father on the other hand, maintained his skeptical expression, which pissed her off all the more. She had half a mind to take Caleb down to the dock and give him a blowjob he'd never forget, just to teach her dad a lesson. But of course, her dad would never know even if she did. And then she'd never get rid of Caleb.

It came as a surprise, but away from her parents, Caleb actually proved to be more of a real person. Less stiff and formal, he even made her laugh a time or two. But she was loyal to John, and nothing was going to change that.

At least that was the case, right up until their anniversary came and went without a single word. It wasn't their real anniversary, because they'd kind of just fallen into couplehood, and neither could put their finger on an exact date to call their beginning. But Emily did know the exact date she gave up her virginity to John in that hotel room up at Pine Key.

Two days later a letter finally arrived. Short and sweet, the letter took her breath. The words *Forget me*, and *You should move on* brought hot, wet tears. Before they'd even dried, the heat turned to anger. All she'd ever done was love John the best way she could, and just like that, without any explanation at all, he was telling her to move on. Well move on she would.

She felt guilty, when she left Caleb's. Even more so than she had that first time with John, but no way was she going to confess such a sin to the priest. She woke up that Friday morning and prayed her rosary three times, said half a dozen Hail Mary's and wrote John a letter. It was a pathetic missive of longing and despair and even she knew it. Still, she sealed the envelope. As her tongue touched the sticky, glued edge, her mind betrayed her and drifted back to where it had been the night before. She pushed Caleb from her mind and set off for the post office.

As she walked through the door and stepped into line, she found Captain Rick in front of her. They chatted for less than a minute before he pointed at the letter in her hand. "You hear from him much?"

Emily wilted instantly. Tears welled uncontrollably as she fought back a sob, "No, hardly ever."

"Come on, Kiddo." He led her out of the line. "Let's grab some coffee."

She nodded and gently pressed back the tears in the corners of her eyes. Captain Rick pulled out a red bandana and offered it to her saying, "Take it. I promise it's clean." His laugh felt easy and natural, so she did exactly as he suggested.

At the coffee shop around the corner, Mike Herrera handed Emily an oversized coffee mug. The foam on top of her caramel latte had been poured and shaped into a little heart, which nearly made her start crying all over again. Emily had known Mike since Middle School, when he sat beside her in the clarinet section of the band. She didn't want anyone else to see her cry, so she thanked him and walked to the table. "Why doesn't he write me? I send at least one letter every week."

Captain Rick touched her hand and said, "John is looking for something he hasn't found yet. He was looking long before he left Key West. He might be the best I've ever seen at spotting things out on the horizon, but he never was worth a damn at noticing the things right at his feet. Lord knows he comes by that honestly."

The mug in his hand gave off steam, and for a second or two Captain Rick seemed to drift off with it. After a moment he looked at her and said. "His choices aren't yours. I'm going to tell you the same thing I told him before he left. I've seen a lot of life, and one thing I've learned—life is only made of all you've got to lose."

Emily frowned unsure what he meant, but again Captain Rick looked off into something unseen for a moment, so he didn't notice her puzzlement.

Finally, he said, "The world is yours to make of it what you will. The hardest part, and the beauty of life, is that every damn thing comes down to the choices you make. As we sit here, you can make choices to continue doing everything exactly the same way you have been." He took a drink of coffee before arching one of his gray eyebrows that reminded her of a caterpillar. "Or on the other hand, you could stand up and walk out that door, hellbent to quit putting your life on hold for somebody else's choice. Change the whole future."

"Are you telling me to forget John?"

"Nope. That's your decision to make. But take it from an old man who's seen an awful lot in this world, you got one chance. Even if you buy into the sales pitch of a heavenly ever after, you still only have the one shot at life on this planet. So live the best one you can...for you. And you alone. Only you know what that looks like. And when you look back, you won't regret the choices you made, probably not even the mistakes. What you will regret, is the time you wasted doing nothing. You'll regret the energy and work and love you wasted on things and people you only thought you wanted. Trust your gut. You know what feels right and what feels wrong. Learn to cut and run when you need to. That's what'll keep you sane in this world."

That evening Emily's mother took her out for dinner. The place was packed, so they had to wait for a table.

"Let's order some wine at the bar."

Her mother ordered two glasses of Chardonnay, which tipped Emily off that she wanted to talk about Caleb. They stood at the crowded bar, sipping the cool wine.

"These tourists are the bane of my existence," her mom said. "Almost makes me miss Buckhead." No sooner had the words left her mouth than two young college boys walked up, loud and obviously sloppy drunk.

"Hello ladies," the first said with what must have struck him as a suave wink. He looked them both up and down, but his gaze settled on her mom as he said, "Damn you got a nice ass, girl."

Her mom held up her ring finger to show a sizeable diamond and said, "Thanks, but I usually call him my husband."

Emily laughed as the host walked up to seat them.

They chatted all the way through dinner, before her mother finally brought it up. "How are things between you and Caleb?"

"Okay, I guess," Emily remained cautious..

Her mother smiled warmly. "I'm not trying to push anything on you. I just hate seeing you sitting around the house, waiting on a boy who doesn't even write back."

"Things are just kind of weird right now I guess."

"Honey, it's your life, so if you think they're weird, maybe you need to reassess and do what doesn't feel weird. For you."

Emily thought back to her conversation with Captain Rick. The two girls finished their evening, thankfully without another mention of the situation at hand. For the first time, they seemed more like girlfriends than a mother and daughter, and Emily was thankful.

Summer arrived some three months later and still Emily hadn't received another letter from John. The days and weeks slid by, and Emily still felt like she was just being carried by the current.

To celebrate her nineteenth birthday, Caleb took her for a sunset cruise on his catamaran. The July sky was brilliant. They were having a good time, and as the sky turned to fire over the Caribbean, Caleb pulled a small, white, satin box from his pocket and knelt in front of her.

Maybe she loved him in that moment. Maybe she was just caught up by the perfection of the setting sun over the water. Maybe she simply wanted something different for her life. Whatever the reason, she said yes.

Six weeks later Emily heard the news. John was in Germany. Alive but lucky to be, so the rumors said. John had lost both legs and one eye. Others in his truck hadn't been as fortunate.

Emily didn't leave her room for three days.

Even injured, he was no more reachable for her. She struggled with what felt like a hurricane of feelings, torn between love, guilt, anger. But John had moved on ages ago. Besides she was engaged to another man. She talked to her priest about the feelings she still had for John, even as she planned a Spring wedding.

Come February, Emily found herself staring into a full-length mirror at the bridal boutique, when Captain Rick's words came back to her. Her final fitting before the wedding, and it all suddenly felt so wrong. There was no joy in this. Not like it was supposed to be, when a girl finds love and gets her dream wedding.

The saleswoman left them alone for a few minutes, when Emily began to cry.

"Honey, what's wrong?" Her mother touched her shoulder, but it was Bethany, her Maid of Honor to be that took charge.

"Let's get you out of this thing." She started undoing the hooks down the back

Bethany had been Emily's best friend since kindergarten. She might spend most of her time on the other side of the country now, in school at Pepperdine, but she was here for this fitting and anytime Emily needed to talk. They logged hundreds of minutes on the phone each month and countless texts, but still Emily had never confided her rising angst about marrying Caleb.

Nevertheless, Bethany seemed to understand the situation. As soon as they got Emily dressed in her regular clothes, Bethany said, "I got this Mrs. Atwell. I'll text you in a bit." She led Emily out of the dress shop.

They drove over to the other side of the island without speaking a word. Staring east over the vastness of the blue water Emily said, "I don't think I can do this."

"Nobody says you have to. You can call it all off right now."

"My parents have already spent a fortune. I'd be letting them down. Besides, it would be devastatingly embarrassing." She turned and stared at Bethany. "Like the worst thing ever. I'd be the gossip of the whole island."

"Probably. But the worst thing ever, would be marrying a man you don't really love. Especially if you get stuck on this tiny strip of land with nowhere to escape. That would definitely be worse than being the island gossip for a few weeks."

The waves rolled in one after another. Emily watched

them for a while before she said, "I'm late."

"Late? Like you had an appointment to be somewhere, or late like holy shit, I'M LATE?"

"The holy shit variety."

Bethany exhaled loudly before asking, "How late?

"Three weeks and two positive tests late."

"Holy shit. This is really bad, Emily."

"That's comforting to hear."

"I'm here for you, Em. Does Caleb know? Your mom?"

Emily shook her head. "No one knows. Except you."

"Come back to Cali with me. You can clear your mind without all the other pressure. We can figure it out there without your mom and Caleb breathing down your neck."

That night Emily packed only a carry-on bag. She sneaked away to the airport, without telling her mom or anyone else she was leaving. She simply didn't have the energy for goodbyes and all the questions that would come with them. She bought a one-way ticket to Los Angeles. She wouldn't be around for her father to be angry about the credit card bill.

He canceled the card before her plane had even landed. She figured that out, as soon as she tried to make a withdrawal at LAX. She had sixty-three dollars cash and the support of one good friend. The rest she had to figure out for herself. She'd never felt so alone in her life.

Weeks later, Bethany loaned Emily the money she needed and gave her a ride. She sat there by her side and tried to convince Emily she'd somehow feel better afterward. But Emily felt worse. The guilt consumed her. And not the Catholic kind of guilt with the bleeding Jesus hanging on a wall between stained glass windows, to remind us what terrible people we all are. She felt real guilt. She truly was a terrible person. At least in her mind.

She distracted herself with the non-stop parties of LA. The free-flowing alcohol and pot, helped erase the thoughts … until they weren't strong enough. Cocaine and Molly became her new counselors. Neither helped her bond with Bethany. Nor did the boyfriend she found. Soon she was staying with him in the filthy, little bungalow out by Venice Beach. Emily torched bridges, drowned relationships, and burned up a year. A year in which she ignored what must have been hundreds of texts and calls from her mother.

Honey please call me or text. At least let me know you're ok.

I'm ok.

But she wasn't okay. She was merely, barely, existing.

She didn't text back often, and she never called, but the occasional text seemed to be enough to keep her phone on. Emily guessed they feared her disappearing all together.

She would if she could. But even here, about as far from Key West as she could get, the tiny island mocked her. Not a day went by that she didn't think about it. Here the countless street vagabonds reminded her of stray cats and the gypsy chickens back home, scratching around for restaurant scraps. She missed the smell of her mom's roses mixed with the fresh, salty air.

But she couldn't go back. Not until she got her shit together and she couldn't seem to get her shit together. Not way out on the wrong coast. Not trying to handle everything on her own.

She got sick of the drugs and the crowded, messy heap of guys crashing at the house by the beach. So she dumped her latest guy, quit smoking, and limited herself to a couple two or three drinks most nights. She found a job at a coffee shop off Sepulveda. The money was shit, and she stayed broke. But she snagged a bed in a tiny apartment shared with two other girls she found on Craigslist. Even splitting the place, rent was insane here in California.

A couple of questionables claimed they could get her an audition or a part in some new series. Everyone assumed she'd left Key West to chase an acting dream, and that seemed better than the truth, so Emily let the lie breathe. But she saw what became of the girls that ended up on a casting couch.

Her one roommate danced at a club a few blocks over, and Emily thought about giving that a shot, but she was too damned white and awkward to make much of dancer. Her roommate said the men with the money didn't come for the dancing. But Emily already harbored enough guilt and shame, so she stuck with serving the world hot coffee and cold shoulders.

No one here seemed to notice. She liked it that way, after the wake of heartache she'd left behind.

Her father had spent twenty grand on a wedding she'd ditched. She left her mother feeling guilty and wondering what she'd done wrong to drive her away. She knew this from the texts that came in. She'd left Caleb practically at the altar. He'd sent her some truly awful texts, but she deserved every word.

John was apparently in physical rehab somewhere in Texas. That fact she'd learned from Captain Rick. She only called him the once, and if he knew about her disappearing act, he never let on.

But her greatest guilt remained in the choice that brought her here to California. Sometimes when she had more to drink than she should, Emily looked at the picture she'd downloaded of a baby at eleven weeks gestation. Twice, in the dead of night, when she couldn't sleep, Emily left the apartment and climbed the stairs to the rooftop of the building. She stood there on the edge of the parapet and felt the wind blow against her face.

She looked west, imagining she could see the ocean waves from her perch high up in the city, but she couldn't see much of anything but lights, smog, and despair. She thought about taking that one last step, but what would her mom say if she committed the one sin that offered no chance of forgiveness?

There on that ledge, she could almost smell her Momma's roses and somehow that scent kept her feet firmly planted.

Never in all the months did her dad call or text, until that night.

Call me Emily. It's about your mother. 911

Her gut told her his message was no ploy.

"Your mother collapsed in her garden three days ago. She's been in the hospital. You need to come home. She has cancer. In her pancreas. The doctors say it will go fast from now to the end."

Less than twenty-four hours later Emily, landed in Key West, carrying only the duffle bag she'd left with. Her dad hugged her tight and didn't ask a single question. They talked only about her mom and the grim news from her doctors. She spent the first three days beside her Momma's bed, but by the fourth day she had to escape. With no place really to go, she wandered into the same coffee shop where she and Captain Rick once had their talk.

Mike Herrera stood behind the counter. Just like before. "Caramel latte?" he asked as if she'd been in only the day before.

"Yeah, that'd be great. You still working here, huh?" She cringed realizing that the observation was not only obvious, but smacked of condescension. She hadn't meant anything by it. After all she had no room to criticize anyone for their lot in life.

Mike smiled and shrugged. "Actually, I own it now." The machine hissed as he steamed her milk. "Technically the bank owns it, but I saved enough for a down payment to buy my old boss out when he retired."

"That's awesome. Sorry, I didn't know. I've been gone a while."

He nodded, and she could tell he knew at least something about her disappearing act. Her mug came with the same heart as before, and again the sight of it almost made her cry. Except she was nearly out of tears after so many days of uncontrollable weeping. He waved off her attempt to pay for the drink.

The place was dead and she really didn't want to sit alone with her thoughts so she looked at Mike and asked, "Want to join me?"

"I'd love to." He grabbed a bottle of water and walked around the counter.

When he sat across from her she forced a smile. "I've been working in a coffee shop too. In LA, but I never have gotten the hang of Latte Art."

Mike laughed and raised one eyebrow. "It's an ancient Chinese secret."

Emily chuckled, "But I'm not sure what to make of a true coffee artiste, who does not drink his own concoctions." She tried to ladle on a French accent, but wound up sounding more like Count Chocula.

He held up his water as a toast, and she touched the side of her mug to the plastic bottle.

"Actually," he said. "I probably would've made myself a cup but I was more interested in sitting with you."

"That's sweet."

He grimaced.

"What's that look for?"

"Sweet." He looked down at the table with a sideways smile. "Some things never change. Mike Herrera, Lord of the Friend Zone."

She chuckled at his candid assessment. He was right. She knew he'd had a bit of a crush on her since middle school. He'd always been kind of a nerdy. But he was a great guy. A guy she'd always thought of merely as a friend.

"I can't believe I'm back here," she said. "I came back because my mom." She choked back tears. "She's sick."

He nodded. "I know. Small island. I'm really sorry. She's a super nice lady. We always talked about you, when she stopped in. She brought me a rose bush, when my dad died. Told me where to plant it and how to take care of it and stuff. She said for the rest of my life I could think of him, when it bloomed. She's pretty amazing."

"I'm sorry Mike. I had no idea your dad died."

"Heart attack. He was fishing with his buddy. Hooked a big Marlin and well, I guess the fish won. I bet he's up in heaven right now griping about the one that got away."

That brought a genuine smile to Emily's face. She loved the fact Mike could put a positive spin on such a sad fact of life. It made her open up about her mom. "I don't know what I'm going to do. My dad either. She holds that whole house together." Emily's eyes filled with tears. "Even when I was gone, she somehow kept me going. I let everybody down, screwed everything up, but her love for me was so strong anyway. It's like it reached across the country and kept me safe. I kind of hated roses all of my life, but sometimes, when I was really struggling, I swear I could smell them in the air."

Over the next few months Emily's mother had good days and bad days, but mostly she slept. Emily took over the Rose garden and kept it as beautiful as ever. On the good days, she helped her mother come outside and they sat on the bench together, amid the fragrant blooms.

Her father promoted one of the managers at the office to vice president and gave up much of his responsibilities, so he could spend more time at home. His former harshness seemed entirely gone. Not once did he so much as bring up her absence or anything about the difficulties of the past. The love he had for his wife, and for Emily, overshadowed all else, though it sometimes seemed as if her mother's cancer would claim him too.

Emily made him eat at least one meal a day, and she busied herself with keeping up the house and garden. Little by little, she took over most of her mom's old duties. Emily and her father even began to find little things here and there to laugh about. But still, Roger Atwell was a man struck numb by the impending death of his one true love.

Emily returned to the church where she grew up, mostly out of grief and fear regarding her mother. But soon she took over her mother's time slot for adoration, and it was in this weekly hour of silent reflection that she found a quiet place for her grief to reside. She thought about her mom, her dad, and even John, who she heard was working through learning to use replacement legs, like so many other soldiers these days. She prayed for Caleb and Bethany and all the other people she'd wronged or disappointed. And she prayed for Mike, who had her coffee waiting each time she left the church.

Sometimes she thought back to that day at the shop with Captain Rick. He'd been right about one thing. What she regretted most was the wasted time. The time she spent away from her mother.

Emily smiled when she could, because her mom asked her to. Smiles seemed to come most easily when Mike happened to stop by. Every so often, he delivered coffee to the house. Even on the tough days, Mike could draw a little grin, maybe even a laugh from Emily. And that never failed to bring a smile to her mother's face as well.

He was sweet and sincere. And though he didn't seem to have to go out of his way to be so. Mike talked about his dad, and grief, and her mom's cancer, without the platitudes others handed out. When he was beside her, Emily felt like she could survive this storm, even her Momma's passing. He entertained her with stories of the ridiculous goings-on at the coffee shop, from the whacky locals, to drunk tourists acting like idiots, to Celeste, the flamboyant trans lady who came by almost daily to try and talk Mike into "trying a new flavor." Emily laughed until her sides hurt. And when there was nothing to say, he would just hug her. Wrap his arms around her and let her cry and get it all out.

Her mother persisted, and even as her body withered, her spirit was interminable. She spent every day telling Emily about relatives, and her childhood, and lessons she had learned. Things she wanted Emily to always remember when she was gone. They laughed and they cried, and they both tried to squeezed a lifetime into those months.

On a Thursday in July, Mike stopped by after his morning shift, as he did most every day now. He walked through the front door without knocking and found Emily sitting next to a to-do list, in back, on the veranda.

"I brought you a latte with extra caramel."

"You always bring me a latte," she laughed. "You're gonna make me fat."

"You'd still be beautiful, and I'd love you just as much."

The two of them stopped and looked at each other. Neither of them had said the word yet.

Sheepishly, his lopsided grin spread across his now crimson tinge cheeks. She didn't know when it had happened, but in that moment, he looked like the most handsome man she'd ever seen. Emily calmly stood up, took the coffee cups from his hands and set them on the table beside them.

Mike wasn't the timid middle school boy she'd kept in her mind. He stood there in front of her, strong, loving, and compassionate. She laid her hands against his chest, and he responded by wrapping his arms around her waist. They looked at one another for just a moment longer, and closed their eyes. Sweetly and gently, they kissed.

Two weeks later, the home health aides helped Roger and Mike set up a bed outside, in the middle of the rose garden.

Emily Atwell married Michael Herrera, standing under an archway of climbing roses, there in the backyard, amid the fragrance of her Momma's roses.

It wasn't the big church wedding she'd once planned. Still it felt right, and perfect, and full of joy. And if her mother was weak with cancer, no one there would've ever known. She beamed like an angel with pride, alongside her husband, Roger. Mike moved in, so that Emily could spend the time she needed with her mother, and he could be there for her at night.

Two weeks later, on Sunday, Mike's one day off, he sat holding Emily's hand on the veranda, talking about the week ahead. Her father came walking out the screen door. It was obvious he'd been crying. "Your mom wants to talk to you for a little bit," he said as he patted her shoulder and rubbed his eyes with the other hand. "I'm going up to the church."

Emily stood somberly and walked past her dad into the house. She opened the door to her mother's room and a soft voice said, "Come here to me, baby."

As she walked to the chair by her mother's side, she saw the pile of crumpled tissues, on the bedside table where her father had been crying. A knot grew in Emily's throat. Her father had always remained strong and cheerful by his wife's side.

"Momma, are you okay? What's going on?" Emily was afraid to even speak.

"Honey, it's going to be okay. I won't be around much longer. I can feel it, but I want you to know I'm at peace."

Tears flowed freely down Emily's cheeks and dropped from her chin. "Momma, I don't want you to go," she cried.

"Baby, we all have to go sometime. It's going to be okay. I'll never really leave you Emily. Remember, you're my favorite flower and the most beautiful thing I've ever created."

"Mom, I can't do this without you," Emily sobbed.

"You won't ever have to. I'll be here. Think of me

every time you see a rose bloom. I want you to know I'm proud of the woman you've become. And you've got Mike now. He's such a good man, honey. You're so blessed to have him. And I'm thankful you're here to take care of your father. He's going to be a mess, and between me and you he'd lose his ass if it wasn't sewn to the top of his legs."

Emily laughed for a brief second, but her tears kept flowing.

"Emily it's going to be okay, my sweet girl. I will love you forever."

Teresa Atwell passed away gently in her sleep later that day.

At the funeral, Emily stood strong as family and friends shuffled by to pay their respects and give their condolences. Mike held her hand and stood firm on one side, her father on the other. Together they got through the day and the weeks that followed. Each morning Emily woke early with Mike, and after he went to open the coffee shop, she made breakfast for her dad, before she tended to the roses.

This was the routine that carried her through those first months. She was pruning a row of young bushes, when she noticed a new bloom just beginning to open. The tender, new petals were a deep shade of purple, darker than any of the other flowers. This was one of her mom's grafts, so she pulled out her log book to read her mother's notes. The familiar script made Emily miss her all the more, but she was so grateful for this cata-log of writings. Every page a reminder of her mother's legacy.

She read the notes her mom had made about experimenting with a new combination of varieties. She thought about the love and care her mother put into each of these flowers she loved so much. Emily blinked a moment as the warm greenhouse began to spin, and the words on the page blurred. She realized just in time she was about to be sick. Afterward, Emily sat on the bench outside the greenhouse trying to quell her nausea. She inhaled deeply smelling the bouquet around her, but try as she might she didn't feel quite right until later in the afternoon.

That night in bed, she told Mike about the beautiful, purple rose her mother had created, how unique and lovely it was. Then she told him about the vertigo and getting sick. "That's strange," he replied. "Take it easy in this heat, okay?" She didn't say anything else to Mike that night. But she knew it wasn't the heat.

The next morning, after she made her way to the drugstore and back, she wanted to call the coffee shop but she waited and instead walked out to the garden. Inhaling the familiar scents deeply, she pushed open the greenhouse door. Emily bent to smell the magnificent, new purple bloom. The aroma was fresh and rich and made her smile. She cupped her hands around the rose and held it gently and said, "Guess what, Momma?"

Bloom
by Dan Johnson

Momma said bloom where you're planted.
Make the place you are your home.
She said, what if my seed landed,
Where flowers won't grow from a stone?

They said, you ought to count your blessings.
There's far worse places you could be.
She said, if this is where God put me,
Then let an angel spread her wings."

She said I can fly. I won't touch the ground.
I need to climb high and take a good look around.
You'll stay in my heart, wherever I may go.
But it's time for me to leave here and find a life to call my
own.

Dreams are a whisper in the darkness.
She fumbled 'round to find her way.
She called her mom, when she got scared to death,
But only said, she was doing okay.

She knew they'd catch her if she stumbled.
She had to do this by herself.
She'd rather trip on her own feet,
Than hold their hands and ask for help.

She said I can fly. I won't touch the ground.
I need to climb high and take a good look around.
You'll stay in my heart, wherever I may go.
But I gotta keep trying to make a life to call my own.

Real life happens quickly.
It'd been years since she'd been home,

When Daddy called, said Momma's sick, babe.
The doctor says she don't have long.

So she held her Momma's frail little hand.
She said I wish I hadn't gone.
But Momma said you did the right thing,
I'm proud of the woman you've become.

But I've got to fly. I won't touch the ground.
I need to climb high and take a good look around.
You'll stay in my heart, wherever I may go.
But it's time for me to leave here,
'Cause this old world, it's not my home.

She said Momma fly. Don't touch the ground.
I'll meet you on high. We'll have so much to talk about.
You'll stay in my heart, wherever I may go.
And I'll see you when that day comes. You'll always be
my home.
I'll see you when that day comes.
'Cause Momma you've always been my home.

Ice Water

Inspired by the song "Tom Waits for No One" by Dan Johnson

A boat's no place to wait for somebody. Ain't no place to live either, but here sits my dumb ass doing both. God, what a fucking fool.

Anger is a costume other feelings wear. His heart quivered like a clapboard house in the hurricane. Ripped apart and scattered he wanted to hold the pieces together but he was coming apart. Still his pride clung to what he recognized was a futile effort. He'd damn sure been involved in enough of them.

Crushing a cigarette butt out on the bottom of his boot, he threw it in a coffee can already half-full from the day's stress.

Maybe I should've fought more for the house. But fuck, it's not like I left her any choice. Martha had to kick me out. Hell, I wanted her to do it.

The house was on Virginia Street, nice place, not too far from the marina. When Rosie used to sneak over to his boat, he'd sing her that old Tom Waits song and change it to Virginia Avenue to match the lyrics. He'd also change the line about the crazy lizard in his brain, to the crazy lady in his old house. Rosie would laugh, and the sound poured joy into his hard, old heart.

Martha had kept the house. He'd kept the boats. Probably a better deal than he deserved. And he'd wanted it that way. His desire for Martha was long gone, and that had been the case even before Rosie. Though he'd admit it chapped his ass that Stoney, the old, hippie bastard, now spent his nights in the house with Martha, his long, stringy hair strung across the very pillow he'd once called his own. Never mind Rosie had often stopped by his boat to lay her thick, black hair across pillowhe once shared with Martha.

Goddamnit, Rosie.
She's not coming. Godamnit, I'm a fool.

Tonight, Rosie was supposed to come back. That's what she'd said, and what he kept telling himself every day since. He would've bet every boat he owned on it. Problem was, he was a piss poor gambler. He could fish better than any of them, but more than once he'd lost his ass on card games and slow-footed horses. A man who knows how to work can lose money and always make more. Tonight, he'd lost so much more than that.

"A fucking break she said," he said aloud, though

not a soul was in earshot.

I should've smelled the stink of that lie when it fell out of her mouth.

"Give me a month to sort things out at home…It's too hard going back and forth between the two of you. I need to figure out what's best for me," he mimicked her pouty face, and thick accent.

Fucking brush off is what it was. Choosing that asshole. Again. That's what the fuck this was. She couldn't just tell me the damn truth? Hell no. Left me to read the goddamn writing on the wall.

"I'm real goddamn glad you can figure out what's best for you! Because you're fucking killing me!" His shouts echoed around the still marina.

Picking up his wine glass, he walked to the top drawer by the bed and pulled out the stack of letters from Rosie. Beneath the envelopes and folded scraps of paper sat the old silver coin he'd carried all these years. He read through each missive again, like he'd done a hundred other times. So many passionate professions of love. So many promises of "some day." He finished another glass and leaned over, pulled the coin from the drawer and put the letters back.

He'd won the coin in a boxing match back in Cuba, when he was a young man. He was small then, but scrappy. Most of the bets were against him. But an older man with a thick, round, white beard placed a bet on him. It would be some time before he figured out who the old man was.

His opponent was a big, barrel-chested, brute with cauliflower ear, swelled till it looked like it could pop. And when he'd won the fight by knocking out the brawler opposite him, the old man laughed aloud and collected his winnings.

"There's fire in you, boy," the old man had said. "I can see it. Hang on to this." He had tossed him the old coin. "I picked it up hunting the Badlands of the Dakotas. The old Indian that traded it to me said it came off the battlefield at Little Bighorn. Keep fighting son. Take what you want from this world." And then the asshole walked away with the very girl Rick had been cozying up to the nights he spent in Havana.

He'd hung onto the coin all these years, refusing to sell it even at his financial worst. He assumed with its age, and who gave it to him, that the thing was probably worth some money. He'd promised Rosie he'd sell it and use it to sail away with her. He flipped the coin a couple times and shoved it in his pocket. Grabbing his wine glass, he walked back to the galley, still thinking about her.

I should've eaten that Yellowfin, if I was gonna drink all this damn wine. Burnt to a crisp. And those worthless fucking linen napkins.

He'd gone out of his way today, to fish for the Yellowfin and had "borrowed" a set of table linens from the new chop house down on Duval.

Here in the end, none of it meant a shittin' thing. Know what I miss most? My goddamn pride.

Tick. Tick. Tick.

Here I sit, drunk, pissed off, sad, and lonely. Living on a fucking converted fishing boat. The love of my life gone. And all I can do is sit here and try and convince myself she's just late.

"Dammit Rosie why? Why do you have to do this to me?"

Tick. Tick. Tick.

The cheap, plastic clock on the wall counted off the seconds, almost keeping time with the water slapping against the hull. The water didn't bother him much. He had no delusions of controlling the tides or the waves.

But the clock. He swore the damned thing was mocking him. A man ought to have some say over time. He'd picked the night, the time, thinking he was setting himself up to sail away with her into the rising sun, come tomorrow.

A break. She needs a break so she can make up her mind. She needs to work on her, before she can be good for me.

"What a crock of shit!"

I get it. She's got to choose between us. And I know how much is tying her down. But I know how much she loves me. And she has to know how much I love her. She needs time ...

"I need some fucking luck!" He pounded his fist on the counter, sending cheap silverware scattering to the floor.

Father Time and Lady Luck. Sounds like a song. Like a man's got any control over either damned one. Neither one sails for my fleet, that's for damn sure.

Jesus. Shut the hell up, dumbass. You know why you can't keep your shit together, or keep a woman around? Because you think you're some kind of goddamn fisherman poet. Idiot. Where'd I put my damn smokes?

Tick. Tick. Tick.
Tick. Tick. Tick.
"Fuck you clock!"

What am I Captain Hook? Talking to clocks. Running from time like a goddamn crocodile?

He slapped the clock off the wall. It skittered and settled atop his bunk, right next to the pillow Rosie used when she used to come by.
Tick. Tick. Tick.
"Fine, have it your way." He grabbed the clock and walked out onto the stern. He started to pitch the damn

thing overboard, but he didn't want to think about it down there in the green waters, still keeping time. So he popped the two little batteries out first.

They didn't even give a satisfactory splash, when he dropped them over the side.

He flung the now silent clock across the slip just to hear it crash land on one of his charter boats.

Let the fucker who takes that one out tomorrow wonder how the hell a clock got on deck. They won't ask though. Even if they recognize it's mine. My men know better than to ask me stupid questions.

"This is my motherfucking fleet!"

My charter service. Built from nothing. All by myself. Captain Rick!

"Fuck 'em! Fuck 'em all!"

The wine and the anger were bellying up to each other, squaring off, somewhere between a fight and a dance.

She's with him right now. I know it! Sitting at their table together? Getting ready for bed? Making their own kind of waves? I bet he's banging her right now.

The anger convinced him she was with the husband she hated. The wine filled in the details. "You're ripping my heart out Rosie," he whispered this last thought but still it rang loud inside his head.

God she's so sexy. So smooth and brown, when I put my big hands around her waist. The way my light skin looks on top of her dark skin. And those curls of hair that hang down in her face when she looks up and gives me those deep, black eyes. I'd rip my heart out of my chest and hand it to her to hold forever. If she'd just take it.

He couldn't stand the thought of that little asshole fucking her right now. The bastard didn't deserve her.

When she stands there in her sundress with that coy little smile. And slips her arm behind her and unzips it, to let it fall to the floor. Her naked, little body is so beautiful. The curve of her hips. Her flat, supple belly. Those breasts so round and firm and perfect.

He loved to stand behind her and trace his finger across her shoulder blades and down her back. To feel every little bone nestled between the muscles. To stop on that perfect curve just above her ass.

Oh my god her ass. She can't go back to him. I can't lose her.

If he was lucky, the boy was keeping them up. Maybe he'd have a nightmare and sleep in bed between them.

Maybe he was sick, and thats why she couldnt come tonight.

With that hope, that convenient little lie, he turned the stereo back on. He'd shut it off an hour ago, when Tom's voice weighed more than his heart could bear. The album seemed romantic, when he'd turned it on. That smooth, jazzy feel. That wailing, muted trumpet. He wanted it playing when she got there. He'd started it over and over. And every time the words sank a little deeper and pinned every ounce of pain to his heart. Now he sat alone, listening yet again.

Had he stepped off the boat and walked toward town, he'd have found Rosie, not in the arms of the man he hated, but a hundred feet from him. By the gate to the pier.

‡‡‡

He remembered the first time he saw her, sitting in a corner at the Green Parrot, all by herself. December of '88, a Wednesday, the winter solstice. He remembered the details because later, he romantically decided he'd just experienced the best night of his life on the longest night of the year.

Morrison was laying down the "Roadhouse Blues" on the jukebox. Jimmy Flynn was retelling his personal version of "Old Man and The Sea" complete with sharks and "the biggest fucking Marlin you've ever seen." Rick had heard the bullshit story a dozen times over the years, so he sat, sipping a beer, looking around for a good reason to escape.

Damn near every face in the joint he knew. Some worked for him, others bought fish off him, a few he'd invited as "business associates," a long line of creditors. Tonight all of them were drinking on his dime. Captain Rick's annual Christmas Drunkening.

A handful of locals and tourists mingled about. But she was no tourist. Goddamn beautiful is what she was.

Sad too. He could tell that from across the room. He kept his eyes on her for the better part of an hour, while he moved around glad-handing clients, customers, and employees. She wasn't drinking or smoking, odd given the Parrot wasn't the kind of place people came to sit alone and hang out. At first he assumed she was probably somebody's date, but not one swinging dick bought her a cocktail or sat beside her. Though a few did stop to chat her up, not one of them seemed to get anywhere.

A couple of times, he caught her swaying to the music, but mostly she sat still and disengaged, almost glassy, like the flats on a calm morning.

She didn't move a muscle through "All Right Now" or back-to-back Skynyrd tunes, but when Bobby Bland laid down "Ain't No Love," her head kept time to the rhythm while her eyes stayed shut. He paid close attention. She only felt the spirit move her, when the jukebox played the sad, the sorrowful, the beautifully painful songs.

That's the moment he fell for her. She was so young. Too young to know real pain, but he knew she could feel it. Everyone else dances and gets rowdy to a hot guitar or a good beat, but she was moved by the soulful stuff, the good stuff. God, she was amazing.

The Parrot didn't have any Tom Waits on the jukebox, but they did have the Eagle's cover of "Ol' 55" so he played it and waited. He had to outlast Cheap Trick and the Cars before the sad piano started up, and he shifted his eyes her way.

When she started to sway to the tune, he knew he had to take a chance and talk to her. He'd learned life was made of choices that come at you in a flash and leave you behind just as quickly. He wasn't going to let this chance slip by. He took a look around to make sure Martha wasn't lurking nearby. Then he took a seat beside the young woman. Shaking out a smoke, he tilted the pack her way.

She shook him off without so much as a glance his direction. He pulled out the cigarette and stuck it between his lips. "Hope you don't mind if I do."

She said nothing as the Eagles gave way to Bonnie Raitt. Bonnie Raitt was Martha's favorite, so he felt certain she'd played the song. Most likely she was hanging back somewhere, watching him. All the more reason to talk to the dark, sexy woman in front of him.

He and Martha were already through by that point, though neither had admitted it. He was happy to see his mystery girl no longer moving to the music. He might've second guessed his choice and moved on if he'd caught her grooving to Martha's song.

"What do you think?" He asked pointing to the closest speaker. "Is it true?"

"Excuse me?" Her voice carried a sexy Cuban accent.

"This song," I said. "Do you think true love is hard

to find?"

"I wouldn't know."

He smiled. "Great answer."

When she frowned, he added. "That means you haven't found your true love."

"I have all the love I need." The smile she flashed his way held a clear, *So fuck off* message, but damn her lips were sexy.

The waitress came around. Rick ordered another stout then said with a grin, "Get Miss Congeniality here whatever she'd like. Put it on my tab,"

"Ice water please."

He'd been shot down before, but "Ice water please," was a real fucking torpedo. When a woman wouldn't even let a man buy her a drink, he was worse than dead at sea. Marooned, sunk to the cold depths, shipwrecked.

In retrospect, it was the first of countless daggers Rosie would drive into his heart. He hadn't even gotten her name, when he stood and walked away to regroup.

Fucking ice water! Damn she was brutal. He'd had women turn down dances, drinks, and good old-fashioned offers to fuck, but this cold-blooded heartbreaker didn't just turn him down. She cooled him off and sent him running.

He stopped at the bar to intercept the beer. There was Martha talking to Stoney Devereaux. The old Cajun bastard bought a lot of fish off of him, and the stumpy little prick could cook like a motherfucker, but Rick wasn't about to hang around and watch Martha flirt with that coon ass. So he took his beer, drained it in two big drinks, and stepped outside for some fresh air and a smoke.

That's where he found John Rivero, crouched down with his back against the wall, staring down Southard Street.

"Hello Captain."

"What you doing out here John? Get inside and have a drink or ten on me."

He shook his head. "It's too crowded in there."

Rick nodded. The same reason he was standing out here, though for him, just one person had made the place unbearable.

John was smoking a little hand-rolled cigar. Rick didn't know the man very well yet, but he could tell something heavy was on John's mind. John cast Rick a couple of glances, opening his mouth each time only to close it again without saying anything.

"Spit it out, boy."

John's eyes narrowed, and he said, "I am no boy."

"Fair enough," Captain Rick answered. "Then talk to me like a goddamn man."

"I am a better fisherman than Tom Frost."

"Are you now," Rick asked?

John spit out a piece of his cigar. "I grew up fishing these waters with my father. Tom grew up in New Jersey. Let a man of the Keys run your boat, and I promise more fish and happier customers."

"When I hired you on, you told me you'd take any job I had."

"And I did." Rivero stood and folded his arms across his chest. "Now I'm telling you I'm a better captain."

"I'm the fucking Captain."

"*Si*. I meant the Captain of the boat I work on."

John met Rick's stare.

Rick shot the next question at John like a quick, right jab. "So you think I should fire old Tom? Or should I just demote somebody who's worked for me for years?"

John fired back fast. "No, give me my own boat! Let him captain his. See for yourself who is better."

"You're a ballsy little bastard. I'll give you that."

"A man does not get anywhere without taking a risk," John replied confidently.

"How old are you Rivero," Rick asked?

"Twenty-two."

"When I was twenty-two I was running back and forth to Cuba. I took my share of damn risks, and I almost died for them."

"I have never been," John said. "To Cuba I mean. My father barely escaped, and still I have family there, but chances are, I will never see them."

The two stood there a few more minutes, quietly smoking. Sometimes a car passed by, but mostly it was a quiet night, save for the laughter and clatter coming from inside the bar.

John took one last drag from his cigar and pitched it into the street. "Now I am to have a family of my own. My wife told me just tonight that she is pregnant."

"Congratulations," Rick said.

Rivero offered up no thanks, and again the conversation fell into silence, until John finally said, "She is not happy. She blames me. Says I have trapped her here."

Rick had a strong urge to take off walking, but Rivero wasn't finished.

"She wants to leave The Keys. It's too close to Cuba for her. She's not finished running, but if I captained my own boat, how could she say no?"

Rick laughed. "Women always find a way to say no, Rivero. That ain't ever going to change." He took a few steps before turning to face John. "And men. Men like me and you, we're just going to keep on asking for more. Because if we don't, we die, or at least we think we will. We want what we can't have. I'm not sure if I envy or despise those other cocksuckers—the ones that find their finish line and choose to sit back and enjoy life after they cross it. Must be nice."

Rick turned and crossed the street, heading down for the waterfront, before Rivero called out, "What about my boat?"

"You don't have a fucking boat," he called back. "The boats belong to me, boy. But come see me tomorrow."

Ten minutes later, he was standing at the edge of Key West, looking over the dark water out toward the Marquesas. Havana was south of there and just a tick west. He missed Havana like an old lover, though he hadn't laid eyes on her in nearly thirty years. He missed the fights, the characters, the revolution, the guns, and the women. He was drunk. Only when he got good and drunk did he get sentimental, and only a sentimental old drunk missed a place that had damn near killed him.

He blamed the girl back at the Parrot. Those damn sexy lips and ebony eyes. And that accent. There were plenty of Cuban accents in the Keys, but hers wasn't watered down like most. She sounded just like the women back in Havana. The girl at the Parrot was about the same age as those he'd known in Havana. Problem was, he was no longer anywhere near that age.

Chances were she'd seen less than half his years. But a man has to keep dreaming. He'd lived his life on the sea, with the sea. With any luck he'd die at sea. If he stood on land for too long, the sea called to him. His legs needed to be rocked and carried by the waves.

Most likely, the beautiful little devil back at the Parrot had been carried here by the same waves. She'd probably crossed these waters with her family, in some ratty, old boat, hoping they wouldn't drown. Hell, she might've even made the trip on a raft. Either way, she'd battled the sea and a lot of other perils to get here. And in that, they shared something special.

Wrapped in her own thoughts, she hadn't even given him a chance. Blew him off as just another drunk fool making passes at the bar flies. If she noticed him at all, she saw in him the years he'd lived, rather than living he had yet to do. But his finish line was nowhere in sight. He still had worlds to conquer, fortunes to win, and questions to ask. Looking down at his watch, he walked back to the Parrot to ask a few of her before closing time came around.

As chances went, he was ready to take his.

‡‡‡

A room. I should've rented a room. Dammit Rick! You know Rosie hates boats. She's hated them all her life. A smart man would've rented a room.

He sat, pulled the silver coin from his pocket and spun it on the table, thinking about the future he wanted with Rosie. There was nothing he wanted more. He smoked one cigarette after another, as he listened to Tom Waits pour out his soul. His mind wandered, searching for every reason she might not have shown tonight.

> *I know she loves me. She just hates being on the boat. She wants to sit in a windowsill and stare up at a big grapefruit moon. Damnit, what if I got a room now? Let her know to meet me there? She could sit at the window stare at the moon all she wanted.*

He checked his phone again for a message from her. Still nothing. He couldn't call her when she was at home. He could only wait for her to call. She was probably terrified he'd break the rules tonight. He'd pushed the limit just once, because he had to see it. The look on her face showed him how much she feared the confrontation that might someday come.

But he was John's boss, so he made up a quick story about a client complaining. It gave him the excuse to vent his insecurities by chewing John's ass and seeing the tiny apartment. The place had only depressed him—her and him there, with their little family that Rick wanted so badly to have with her.

His old man lived there too. What kind of man still lived with his father? No wonder Rosie was so unhappy.

Even the boy seemed subdued. He'd just turned two at the time, and he sat off in the corner tinkering with some toy, never making a sound.

She loved the kid. She'd been pregnant with him that first night, but Rick hadn't known. He also didn't know she was married to Rivero. Through ignorance or willful blindness, he didn't put that together for some time.

When he'd gotten back to the Parrot, John Rivero was gone. Rosie was still inside, sipping that damned glass of ice water. He'd sobered up on his walk, so he had a clear head when he asked her if she ever wanted more out of life. She wore no ring that night. Or any night since. She was stuck with John, on account of their son, but she hated the man. He was petty and mean, Rick would come to learn from her. But true to his word, the man could fish.

Now the boy was three years old. Rick was torn between envy and resentment. He knew if he'd met Rosie just months earlier, they'd be together. And if the boy were around at all, it would be his instead. He'd be a hell of a better father than John Rivero. And he would love Rosie like John never could.

Fuck love.

From inside Tom crooned, "I hope that I don't fall in love with you." Rick stormed down the steps from the deck, grabbed the turntable, and threw it out the door, onto the stern.

He stood there in the silence, his chest heaving in

anger, but still the graveled voice wouldn't leave his head.

Fuck Tom Waits too.

He came up the stairs in a torrent, grabbed the album from the deck and hurled it out into the darkness of the sea. It sailed so far, he didn't even hear it hit the water.

From behind him a soft Cuban voice came from nowhere. "Rick?"

He spun around, nearly falling over, between the surprise and the wine still polluting his veins. She'd been standing outside on the dock for the last several minutes, working up the courage to walk in.

"Rick we have to talk. I'm leaving."

The split second of hope he'd felt, sank faster there on the water than the batteries or the album. Ice water.

"I don't understand," he said. "You said we'd take a month. You said you'd be back."

"No, Rick. I said I needed time to figure these things out for myself, and I could not do that while you were there in front of me all of the time. I meant what I said. And I have made my decision."

"So what are you going to do? Stay with John and forget all about me?" He couldn't hold back the pain in his heart. It saturated his voice and gained ground toward his eyes by the second.

"No. I'm leaving this place. I cannot spend another day with him. He's a hateful, little man. All he cares about is showing everyone he's better than them."

"Then come with me, Rosie!"

"Rick I cannot stay in this tiny place with him here, especially if I try to go with you. I would be miserable the rest of my life. This could never work. There is no good answer for me here. I'm sorry." She didn't cry. She was firm and cool, and deep inside, Rick knew her decision would not change.

"Rosie, I've wasted the last thirty years of my life, on a business that's bled me dry, with a woman I never loved. So I don't want you living a life that isn't right for you. But give me a chance. Give us a chance!" His voice cracked, and he caught the first tear, with the back of a sun-leathered hand.

"Everything has led me here to you, Rosie. The gun running in Cuba. The ballbusting long hours building this charter service, and the whole damned commercial operation. Hell, even Martha. Somehow it's all led me here to this point, Rosie. Can't you see?"

She spoke more firmly this time. "Rick, I am leaving. I don't love him, and I can't love you. There is no peace here. I need to ask something of you. And I have no right to ask you anything. But I hope out of love for me, you'll do me one favor."

Rick couldn't believe she had the gall to ask anything of him. But they both knew, even as she broke his heart, he would do anything for her.

"I have to leave my son. If I try to take him, his father will fight me, not because he wants him, but because he has to win at everything. I have nothing to fight with, and I cannot be tied to this place any longer."

"So what do you want from me?" Rick was seething. If it were up to him, the three of them would sail away together and never look back.

"Keep an eye on my son, Rick? Make sure he grows up strong and wise, not bitter and petty like his father?"

The request was a square shot to the gut. If she wanted, they could leave together with the boy. But she was ditching them both. Rick had the money to fund her court battle. He'd gladly sell off the boats and the entire operation to move the three of them out of there. She knew that as well.

But she didn't care. She didn't want him the way he wanted her. She never had. He was a temporary escape from a life she hated. Hell, she didn't even want her son enough to fight. All she really wanted was out. And she'd leave him here with an obligation she knew damned good and well he'd fulfill.

"Rick please."

"Go Rosie. Go now. I'll keep an eye on the kid," he spat the words, tasting the wine on his tongue. But the real poison came out last, "I can't make myself stop loving you, as bad as I want to. But I don't want to see you ever again. Some day when you see what a mistake this is, don't bother looking back here. Don't expect to come crawling back, when you realize you've thrown everything you love away...just because you can. You live with this choice and everything it means, from this point forward. Now get the hell off my boat."

Tom Waits For No One
by Dan Johnson

I took the battery out of the clock on the wall,
That ticking was driving me crazy.
I flicked an ash just before it could fall,
Smoked so many the whole room is hazy.
There's two dinner plates out on the table,
A meal that's burned black on the stove.
I've spent hours rechecking my phone for a message,
But I've given up any hope.

Now I'm solo tonight...a bottle of wine,
Two empty glasses with linens pressed fine.
The stereo's on, and I sing along,
A sad lonely song...Tom Waits. Tom Waits for no one.

It's been a month ago Sunday since she said,
She needed some time to reflect.
I haven't seen her nor called her,
Though badly I wanted to,
Waited here with bated breath.

And tonight was the night that she'd promised,
She'd make up her mind and be sure.
Now I've wasted my time, perfecting my lines,
For when she showed up at my door.

Now I'm solo tonight...a bottle of wine,
Two empty glasses with linens pressed fine.
The stereo's on, and I sing along,
A sad lonely song...Tom Waits. Tom Waits for no one.

I'm lonesome tonight. I'm out of my mind.
There'll be no love in this bed made so fine.
She waited so long, as I carried on.
I've come to my senses, but she's come and gone.
The stereo's on, and I sing along,
This sad lonely song...Tom Waits. Tom Waits for no one.

A Bad Man

Inspired by the song "Lone Gunman's Lament" by Dan Johnson

Grady Wayne stared up at cold, hard eyes. He knew better than to challenge his father, but that January wind whistling through the cabin's front door was nearly as brutal as his father, so Grady paused a heartbeat too long.

"You deaf boy? Or just plain stupid? I said go fetch me some fresh straw from the loft. And make sure it's the soft hay," he said, "I don't want no damn sticks poking me."

Grady peered up at his father. His eyes, pleading for understanding he should've known wasn't there. "But daddy…" the back of his father's grizzled, meaty hand crashed down on his ten-year old cheek, spinning his head around and knocking him to the floor. He knew better than to cry. He bore down on the lump that swelled in his throat, and stifled the sobs that needed released. Grady silently picked himself up from the floor and shrugged into the coat that fit snug last winter.

The walk from the house to the barn froze both the snot rimming his nose, and the tears on his cheek he no longer held back. The blistering, biting wind of the high Texas Plains fueled the anger inside young Grady.

"I'll get him some straw. The hardest, godawful, worst straw I can find. Hope it pokes him in his ass all night!" Not that straw would ever hurt as bad as his old man's backhands, or even the brutal insults hurled at Grady, his younger brother, and mother.

The skin on his cheeks burned and cracked beneath the dry, January gusts. Dusty flurries of snow forced his eyes into a tight squint. Grady stepped to the barn door and took hold of the railroad spike used to keep the latch shut. The frigid iron stung his hand, as he grasped the spike and tried to pull it from the eyelet. The two were welded together, by the cold and the ice. The wind blew down his neck and up his sleeves. He yanked with everything he had to free the spike. He couldn't budge it.

His tears began to flow again, freezing before they made it halfway down his cheeks. Pained grunts that came out almost as screams sent his shrill voice skittering with the wind. Failing, or giving up meant another beating. His back still ached from the boot he'd caught just yesterday. The older he got, the more often he felt his father's rage.

Wedging his right hand underneath the sharp side of the spike, he winced as the metal dug into the flesh of his palm, but with one final burst of force, the spike broke free. As it did, his knuckles surged upward, and splinters from the barn door embedded into his hand.

He gasped and cried out in pain, as the spike toppled out and landed in the light dusting of snow at his feet, on the frozen Texas clay.

His cheeks as red as the blood streaming from his knuckles, he squatted to pick up the spike. Rising, he stared at the rusted hunk of iron. Common sense said he should step inside the barn. Instead, he let the cold wind sting him, and that frozen iron burn against his skin. The bloody splinters ached in his fingers, until a calm overcame him. Something about the immediate pain of his physical state relieved, or maybe just distracted him from the unrelenting pain of his life.

He stared at that spike. Cold and hard, like his father. More painful than useful. He gathered the straw for the bed and went back to the house.

Things were quiet when he got back inside. But the old man was in a mood. He'd been pulling on a half bottle of whiskey, and his face grew darker by the moment. The boys' mother sat sewing in the corner, huddled down and withdrawn, in that way she did whenever an eruption from the old man seemed likely. When he got this way, there was only one way the night would end.

Problem was, you never knew just what it was going to be that set him off. Usually nothing at all. Some broken farm tool. A bad patch of weather. Heaven forbid you actually did something to cross him. Like the time his mother burned a skillet full of biscuits, and he'd pressed the hot pan against her skin to teach her a lesson. The bright pink scar still marked her upper arm.

There was the time when Grady was a toddler, and his father snatched him up by the leg for crying. The bones broke under the force, and though the local doctor did his best to set them, Grady would forever walk with a bit of a limp.

The minutes ticked by and with each tip of the old man's whiskey bottle, the tension in the small cabin grew. Still, Grady waited and watched carefully for a sign of the impending explosion. Both he and his mother knew better than to make eye-contact with the surly monster once he got like this. Grady's little brother was young and didn't understand much. But even he sensed the growing anger and kept his head up as he played quietly in the corner. The three could only sit and wait, like the condemned, waiting for the gallows to be built.

And then it happened. His mom got caught looking.

Tonight it would be her.

"What the hell are you staring at!" That's how it began.

"Nothing Joseph. " Her voice cracked as she spoke her husband's name.

"I saw you eyeballing me woman. You got something you want to say?"

"Nothing dear."

"Who the hell do you think you are to look at a man like that?"

"I didn't even mean to look at you." Her voice was strained, though Grady could tell she was trying to sound normal. "Please Joseph, let's just go to bed."

She tried to entice the man to the back room, away from the boys. Though to Grady, it didn't sound like things ever ended much better for her, when the old man took out his frustrations on top of her, behind that door.

"Oh no, I'm curious now. What is it that's so goddamn important?"

"Joseph I don't even know what you're—"

The back of his hand snapped her head back. "I
said speak, woman!"

"Joseph please—"

Another smack from the opposite direction.

Blood trickled from the corner of her mouth. "I
said speak, goddamnit!"

"Please don't do this Joseph. You've been drinking."

It was always worse when he got into the whiskey.
And tonight he was about to polish off the last of the
bottle.

"Who the hell are you to tell me what I can do in
my own house? Damn right I've been drinking! That's
the only way a man can put up with the ignorance I got
to tolerate around this place!" With that he drank the last
swallow in the bottle and threw it at her.

She ducked, and the bottle broke against the fireplace behind her.

Grady's brother James hadn't learned to hold his
wails inside yet. The bottle exploded just above him,
where he sat, drawing stick figures with his finger in the
soot. The boy screamed and started to bawl. Grady knew
his little brother was too close to his father to escape the
boot swinging his direction.

The blow brought only louder sobs.

"Stop that sniveling!" Another kick, this time to the
stomach.

James doubled over in pain wheezing and wailing.

His father lifted a boot above him. Before he could stomp down, their mother dove to cover him.

"Joseph don't!"

The man stumbled backward. "Oh, so now you got something to say?" He grabbed a handful of the soft hair, twisted and pinned-up behind her head.

Still she held on to her young son.

"Thought I made myself clear. Ain't no woman gonna tell me what I can or can't do in my own god-damn home!" He lurched her off the boy. "You got the devil's tongue in you woman. And I ain't going to listen to it no more!"

He dragged her by the hair, kicking and struggling toward the corner. As he stumbled forward, he toed the neck of the broken whiskey bottle. Several inches of jagged glass extended from the base of the neck like a knife. Joseph leaned down and picked up the bottleneck, spinning around to show it to the woman. "I'm gonna cut that Devil's tongue out once and for all."

She screamed as he pressed her head hard down onto the floor and knelt, planting his full weight on her. His knee pinned in the center of her chest, Joseph let loose of her hair just long enough to grab hold of her bottom jaw with his huge left hand. He pressed her mouth open as she struggled to hold it closed.

Grady sat paralyzed.

Every part of him wanted to help his mother. But he'd never been more frightened in his life. The old man dropped the bottleneck to reach into her mouth. His dirty fingers fumbled around, fishing for her slippery tongue as she gagged and choked.

As he finally pulled it far out of her mouth, Grady noticed James. So fixated on the horror unfolding in front of him, he hadn't seen his younger brother muster the strength to stand and pick up the iron poker beside the fireplace. There he was now, drawing the black metal high above his head.

Their father's left hand shot out to grab the bottleneck, their mother screamed, and James swung the iron poker down with every bit of strength the little boy had.

Grady heard the thud as the hooked end lodged in his father's hulking back, deep under his left shoulder blade.

The world moved in slow motion. Grady watched the pain shoot across his father's face, then morph into rage.

For the rest of his life, Grady would never forget the evil in the man's face that night. He'd swear he was looking straight into the face of a demon.

His father let go of their mother's tongue, and his arm swung around and caught James squarely across the chest. The blow launched the boy backward into the wall where he lay face down, stunned from the impact.

The old man rose deliberately to his feet and turned toward the young boy, the poker still dangling from his bloody back. His heavy steps quickened across the room. Drawing close, he brought his knee high in the air, curled his toes toward the sky, and jutted his boot heel out. With all his mighty force, he stomped on the boy. The crunch echoed in the small room.

James' body lay limp.

"No!" His mother's scream pulled Grady back from

his catatonic state. She wailed and crawled toward her son as the old man turned around, the fire of hell still bright in his eyes.

"Do you see what I have to put up with in my own goddamn house?!" He flailed behind his back to grab hold of the iron tool still lodged there. As he pulled the poker free, a squirt of blood shot from the hole. "I'm done with you and these infernal runts!" He walked toward his wife, the iron bar now clutched in his right hand. His left arm hung limp at his side.

Grady remained frozen with fear. He looked over at his brother's unmoving body. A whirlwind of emotions churned in his young soul. It was impossible to tell what was stronger, the disgrace that his brother had been braver than he and suffered so terribly for it, the fear of what his father had in mind, or the need to save his mother. He felt so weak. The shame of that moment would never leave him.

"Grady run," his mother screamed! He looked toward the door, unsure how long it had been since he last drew a breath. His hands trembled as he stretched an arm out to brace himself and rise. But rather than touch the floor, his fingers came to rest on a cool piece of hardwood. His father's Winchester leaned against the wall.

The fear left Grady in that moment.

His hand stopped trembling.

His vision cleared.

And the breath he'd been holding escaped his lungs calmly and easily.

He didn't rush. He didn't even rise. Only moved his

hand to the barrel of the rifle and, placed the stock in his right hand, his finger straightened alongside the trigger just the way he'd been taught.

"Don't put your finger on that trigger until you're ready to pull it," his dad had always warned.

His father continued his slow, deliberate steps toward Grady's mother. Murder in his eyes, he never looked up. Grady leveled the rifle and brought his father into the sights. He pulled back the hammer slowly, two clicks. And only then did the man stop in his tracks.

He turned to look at his son. Evil and rage still contorted his face. Joseph's yellow teeth showed between his lips, as his mouth curled into a smile. You would've almost thought he was looking forward to it.

"Boy. Don't put your finger on that trigger until you're ready to—"

Grady planted a bullet squarely between his father's eyes.

He always was a great marksman.

Grady didn't go to the funeral. He never saw his father again. His mother never married again. And his brother James never walked again.

‡‡‡

Grady dropped his saddle on the ground and leaned against the wall of the bluff to roll a cigarette, as the sun went down in the Western sky, a half day's ride outside Waco, Texas. This was the only part of his chosen career he truly hated.

The waiting.

He had stopped by a small stream to unsaddle his horse and tied it to a Salt Cedar to let it rest and drink a while. He hadn't given the animal a name yet. He never kept a horse long enough to worry much about naming it.

He loosened the sweat soaked kerchief around his neck, as he smoked his cigarette and watched the sun settle behind a hill. He hated the waiting, because of the way his mind would inevitably wander. But he only had two more to go. This would be number ninety-nine.

Whenever possible he liked to wait until nightfall. He was less likely to be seen that way. In fact, in all these years he'd only been spotted a couple of times. Usually Grady was long gone by the time anyone made the connection of who he was, or why he was in town. So he'd wait here until the sun went down. And he would be gone in the middle of the night. With any luck it would be days before anyone connected him with the murder.

Around those parts, the law was administered by a Civil War hero named George Custer. The Army sent him down to keep the peace, as the Union soldiers set up camp across Texas. He had a serious reputation for his particular views on discipline and order. And Grady would just as soon not cross his path.

He tugged at the chain of his pocket watch and checked the time. Another hour and a half or so. Slipping the watch back into its pocket, his fingers touched the silver coin. He pulled it out and looked down at the face. He'd always wondered who that fella was. Some old forgotten ruler he surmised. Rolling the coin between his fingers, he remembered the night he got it.

Grady was sixteen, when he killed his second man. In the six years since he took his father's life, his mother had figured out how to support the family. "Travelers" she called them. Random men who stopped in, stayed for a meal, then spent the night. Some skipped the meal and just left after a quick visit to the back room with his mother.

It hadn't started that way.

She tried to keep things up on the farm, but with only one boy who never really had been that strong, and a crippled younger son who couldn't do anything but sit in a chair, things fell apart pretty quickly. Then one day, just by chance, a man had ridden up on horseback, needing a place to stay for the night. The next day his mother thanked the man. As he handed her some money, she looked down at for a moment. Before he'd made it back to his horse, she rushed out the door after him and told him to be sure and let other travelers know she offered a good place to stay. She spent the rest of the day crying. But a week later, someone else came by.

Years later, one night the noise from the next room had been too much for Grady. He tried to block it out best he could, but the sounds were worse than anything before. The man who showed up at their house that night was a beast. Probably the largest human Grady had ever seen. His mother on the other hand, was a petite woman, slender and a good four inches shorter than her sixteen year-old son.

The noises from the next room tortured him.

And then they stopped.

Grady and his younger brother still shared a small

bed off to the side of the central room in the house. Several minutes later, his mother's door opened. The man looked even larger, looming in the door frame.

As he passed through the room to leave, he looked down and saw Grady's open eyes. He stuck his hand into his pocket, pulled out the silver coin, and flipped it toward Grady, where it landed on the bed. "There kid. Do something good with that. God knows I did some terrible things to your mother." The man chuckled as he walked out the door.

Worried what the man meant, Grady got out of bed and walked to the bedroom door. There lay his mother. Her torn bed clothes and the blood on the bed showed she hadn't been beaten. Just used. She seemed on the very edge of consciousness, whimpering with each shallow breath. Grady threw the covers across her to cover her bare skin. An opium pipe sat on the bedside table. The man had doped her up and ravaged her petite body. Grady opened the drawer in the top of the dresser where he knew she hid a revolver.

Grady walked calmly toward the door.

The man outside was untying his horse from the fence post. "Hey mister."

"What, kid?"

"You're my second..."

That night Grady decided it didn't bother him one bit to shoot a man. He packed a few things, said goodbye to his sleeping brother, and never looked back. By the time he was eighteen, he'd killed two more men.

Killing came easier than anything else in his life. His mind was calm, his aim true. And if he had to admit it, there was something satisfying about taking a life. In every one he killed, Grady saw a bit of his father and a bit of the monster who left his mother near death.

It wasn't long before he was making a handsome living, doing the dirty work of other men. The fat, sweaty gambler in New Orleans. The black fella some banker's wife took a likin' to in St. Louis. The greedy, murdering bitch that took that fella's daddy out with arsenic up in Montana. Somebody always wants somebody dead for one reason or another.

Grady used to ask why. Somewhere along the way, he quit caring.

He'd kept track of the number since the day he'd made up his mind to kill for money, but he couldn't remember exactly when he'd decided to kill a hundred men. He would take the money he'd made, and disappear. Never to deal with the filth of humanity again. This world had given him nothing but hatred and a loose conscience. He'd take the rest for himself. Damn them all.

A hundred seemed like a good round number. May as well stop before the law, or ol' death caught up to him. Tonight, he'd take number ninety-nine.

Almost time to go.

He made his way through cover of darkness up to a small house in the middle of a wide, flat prairie. The rancher who hired him said something about a bad loan or gambling debt. He probably just wanted the land. Grady didn't care either way.

The door stood open in the Texas heat.

Grady walked calmly through the opening and raised his pistol at the man seated across from him. The unlucky fella looked toward the revolver sitting on a shelf beside him.

"Too late mister. You're ninety-nine."

The shot rang out, and the man first lurched violently backward with the force of the slug that entered his chest, then collapsed forward onto the bowl of stew he'd been enjoying seconds before. The satisfying smell of gunpowder filled Grady's nose. A young woman burst through the door beside the dead man.

She screamed, and the infant in her arms began to wail. Grady stood silent, as the sturdy and sun-reddened woman gaped at him. Surprise gave way to fear. Then too quickly, that emotion was replaced with indignant anger. The people in this part of the country were strong and proud. They had to be to survive. She instinctively looked down at the Colt on the shelf beside her.

"Don't," said Grady.

Her determination was not the type to be dissuaded. A small but calloused hand grabbed for the pistol.

"Don't!"

She drew the pistol across her body, the long, black barrel softly reflecting the light of the kerosene lamp on the table. Grady hadn't lowered his revolver. A second shot rang out as he dropped the woman, nearly taking off the top of her head. She spun, stiffened, and tipped over, spilling onto the floor.

"Dammit…that's a hundred."

There would be no money for his last one.

He'd often been tempted to loot a place, after he took care of business.

It'd be easy. But he was no thief. He was a gunman. He had no guilt. Everybody dies—some sooner than others. He just put a date and a number on the inevitable.

He turned to leave in silence.

Silence.

He stopped a moment, turned, and walked to the woman, lying face down on the dusty wooden floor. He wedged his boot heel against her thick hip and shoved. Her limp body rolled, and the baby's tiny body lay on the floor in front of Grady. He knelt beside the child. The flattened shape of its tiny head told him what he hoped he wouldn't see.

Silence.

Grady stood slowly and looked down at the child.

A hundred and one.

He walked out slowly, thoughts he didn't recognize wrestling in his head, and made his way to the horse down by the bluff. He'd saddled her and set things in place for a quick getaway, before his silent stalk to the house. Climbing into the saddle, he paused a moment, and turned back toward Waco.

As he came into town, he glanced up from his thoughts long enough to see a saloon on the right. He tethered the horse and slowly climbed the steps. The doors creaked as he entered. There was a barkeep with his back turned, on the far end of the saloon. The floor groaned under each step, as Grady walked halfway across the empty room.

He pulled a frail, old chair from under a table, warped and stained with age. He didn't plan to drink. He just wanted to sit. The barkeep never turned around.

Grady eased down into the chair and pulled his pistol from the holster on his hip. He placed it on the table and slipped his fingers into his watch pocket. The silver coin was there behind the watch. He drew it from the pouch and held it between his fingers. One side felt warm but the other oddly cool to the touch. He stared down at the face on the coin. "Were you a bad man? Bad as me?"

He spun the coin on the table, under his finger, and the barkeep turned around. His face seemed familiar. Grady watched him work about the bar, slowly wiping out glasses, using only his right arm. His left arm hung at his side, barely useful. The man didn't say a word to Grady. If he'd wanted a drink, he'd have walked to the bar.

Grady heard heavy footsteps on the stairs. A man stepped into the doorway, and the swinging doors spread wide to accommodate his huge frame.

Grady noticed him, but didn't look up. The hulk of a man walked to the bar and got a drink from the bartender. Grady glanced at the men. God that barkeep looked familiar. Grady had walked into so many saloons, in so many cities. He knew he'd seen the man, but lord only knew when or where. His brother suddenly invaded his memory.

He'd done his best to be a good brother to James. The poor kid sat in a chair all day long, mostly staring outside, wishing he could play. His legs were thin and brittle, usually covered with a blanket to keep warm given his bad circulation. But even doomed to a lifetime of being crippled, James was stronger than his brother. Grady hurt for him. "Goddamn the old man for that.

He didn't deserve that grief." Grady wondered what had become of James and their mother.

His mother's sins were many indeed. But he knew they were born from desperation, for the sake of caring for him and his brother. Grady knew his transgressions, on the other hand, were out of greed, malice, and disdain for human life.

Grady dropped the silver coin on the table and pulled his knife from the sheath on his belt. He flipped it around and started scratching words into the table.

Who the hell is that bartender?

It was driving him crazy.

The doors parted and another man entered. Grady saw his bulging sausage fingers wrap over the top of the swinging doors and push them open. The fat man waddled in, his shirt soaked in sweat. Grady knew in an instant who he was looking at. And suddenly, he remembered why he knew the bartender as well.

Grady wondered if he was losing his mind. Or if perhaps somehow the woman in the house had actually shot him, and now he was trapped in his own personal hell. The infant's innocent and lifeless face quickly made its way into Grady's mind.

Damnit! That bitch just had to grab for the gun! Why couldn't she leave it be?

Hell…you'd have done the same thing. She didn't deserve it no more than the young'un. You're a piece of shit, Grady Wayne Johnson.

His own personal hell was exactly what he deserved, if he'd believed in such things. Something inside him felt heavy, hollow, like a sucking void in the deepest pit of him. His stomach turned. Grady carved into the table beside the hammered silver coin, faster, more intently now.

In the next moment another figure appeared at the door, a sharply dressed black man with a confident air. Grady dug his knife deeper into the table, as a knot swelled in his throat. The men gathered in the corner, talking, laughing. They looked over at Grady as he scratched feverishly at the wood.

The door opened again.

A well dressed woman slipped in. Sadness, no, loneliness filled her young, innocent face. Her eyes didn't leave Grady, as she somberly moved across the floor. Grady didn't look up. His chest felt empty. His heart beat faster. The door opened again. One after another, people filed in.

Grady hadn't cried since he was a child. But now, here in this room, his eyes filled. The first drop fell onto the chest of his dusty shirt, and silently, Grady began to weep.

The room was full.

Grady looked around at faces he knew. They all stared at him, seated at his table, bathed in shame. No one spoke. They simply looked at him in silence. He picked up the silver coin on the table and held it flat in his palm, thinking about what he'd done with this life he'd been given.

What was a life like his worth?

The doors slowly parted open one last time.

A man stepped into the room, behind him a strong, thick woman, a baby in her arm. Grady looked up and watched them as they moved across the floor. As they neared, the woman turned her eyes toward him. His tear-stained chest heaved with his sobs, as he lifted his eyes to hers. And the infant began to cry.

Grady lowered his head. He calmly set the coin down and looked at the knife clutched in his hand. He let go his grasp, and it dropped onto the table, as his hand fell to his side.

Grady stared down at the words carved beneath the coin.

FOR TO BURY ME
G.W. JOHNSON

He wrapped his fingers around the pistol on the table and slipped the barrel into his mouth. The satisfying smell of gunpowder filled his nose.

Lone Gunman's Lament
by Dan Johnson

The lone gunman walked in. His stare filled the room.
He sat down in a frail wooden chair.
Surrounded by ghosts of the lives he had claimed,
Save for them wasn't nobody there.

He began to think back how he'd taken each one,
None deserving that cruel fate he brought.
And for the first time the emptiness weighed on his chest.
"Is this how regret feels?" he thought.

For he'd chosen his path in this life long ago,
And he'd never turned back along the way.
And he'd only learned one way to live in this world,
Find what others had and take it away.

As the knot in his throat swelled, he gritted his teeth.
He said I'll be damned if I'll cry.
But he realized just then, he'd been damned long ago,
As the first tear escaped from his eye.
And he sat there confessing a sin with each breath,
To a distant God he'd never known.
While the devil was stoking a flame deep in Hell,
Where he'd one day repay all he owed.

And he knew absolution could never be found,
For the evil he'd wrought on this Earth.
An unseen retribution was all he could give,
as a penance for all those he'd hurt.

He opened his eyes and saw the tears on his shirt,
Where his heart would have been, had he one.
And he'd filled up the void that had always been there,
With remorse for the things that he'd done.

And with no honor to swear on, he swore on his soul.
He would bring no more heartache and strife.
So he prayed for forgiveness for one final sin,
As the lone gunman took his last life.

Thirty Pieces
by Dan Johnson

There's no light without the dark,
No good without knowledge of evil.
No fire without the spark,
And a match in the hand of all people.

And one kiss can change the world,
Count your thirty shekels of silver.
Make your choices wisely friend,
What you'll live, or die, even kill for.

A Digital Copy of the Album is included with your
purchase of this book.

Visit

www.nwdownload.com

and use your personal access code

DJABZHC8VC

Acknowledgments

From Travis ...

I must begin with heartfelt thanks to Dan for trusting me to takes his babies, his characters, his stories and run with them. When done right, a well written song seems like an easy thing, but I know how diffucult of a task it is to take complex things, such as life and hopes, fears and dreams and make them all come alive for a listener or reader.

Without such poignant and emotional source material as a foundation, fleshing out these stories would have been so much harder. If not altogehter impossible. Lucky for me, the stories flowed naturally. Especially Hemingway.

Young Rivero whispered in my ear all the way. Dan, that is a tribute to your character building. Writing these stories alongside you, and with you, was as fun as the creative process gets. The give and take and philosophical discussions over stouts and porters and a whiskey or three was just what I needed most at the time we were creating this project.

Beyond the creative world, you Dan, have been a steady and loyal friend always there when I needed one most. Thanks for all of that.

Ryan McSwain, Monica Pinion, Jonathan Baker, and Mike Akins thanks for your input on these stories and your unique roles in making me a better writer. I miss you guys.

Wes Reeves, like Dan you have been a great friend and there when I needed you. You played a big role in my friendship with Dan. Of course our odd threesome comraderie owes a debt to AJ as he continues to influence our lives powerfuly, even in absentia.

And of course, I must thank my beautiful wife Connie for her unyielding faith in both me and my talents. Life is so much better and easier with you in my corner.

From Dan ...

This project goes out to the families like mine, who have dealt with the pain of losing the one who means everything to you.

If you're worried about someone, be brave enough to wrap your arm around them. Tell them you see where this is leading. Tell them you refuse to live without them. And find them the help they need. From service dogs, to fishing and hunting retreats, to songwriting therapy, and countless others, there are so many effective options out there.

Twenty percent of all profits from the sale of this album and book will forever go to the fight against veteran suicide in America via "Operation Hemingway." Learn the warning signs and help do your part at www.operationhemingway.org.

Thanks for listening.

AUTHORS

DAN JOHNSON IS A TEXAS SINGER-SONGWRITER. HE WAS BORN TO MILITARY PARENTS, ON A BASE IN ITALY AND THEN MOVED TO HIS FATHER'S FAMILY FARM IN BEATTYVILLE, KENTUCKY, WHERE HE SPENT MANY OF HIS HAPPIEST YEARS, WORKING ON THE FARM AND EXPLORING THE MOUNTAINS AROUND HIM. HE GRADUATED WITH A BUSINESS DEGREE FROM WAYLAND BAPTIST UNIVERSITY, AND WORKED AS A BUSINESS AND FINANCIAL CONSULTANT UNTIL LEAVING THAT WORLD TO PURSUE MUSIC FULL-TIME. HE LIVES WITH HIS BEAUTIFUL WIFE, LAUREN, IN FORT WORTH AND SPENDS HIS TIME LOVING HIS THREE AMAZING DAUGHTERS AND ONE EXCEPTIONAL BONUS SON.

AUTHORS

Travis Erwin is an author from Amarillo, Texas. His previous works include a ribald memoir, **THE FEEDSTORE CHRONICLES**, and **TWISTED ROADS** a novel inspired by his appreciation of Townes Van Zandt and many other talented songwriters. His third novel, **WAITING ON THE RIVER** is scheduled for release August, 2018. His work has also appeared in many other literary outlets including Opium Magazine, Underground Voices, and Wide Open Country. He currently lives in Southern California with his wife, and best friend, Connie and a houseful of kids and animals.